"After more than twenty-five years, I'm afraid not even Sherlock Holmes would get very far." He smiled and shrugged at the boys. "On the other hand, who knows? You two could be even better than the great Holmes."

"We'll give it our best shot," Joe said, flashing a look at David and Wishbone.

"My canoe is right over there. "Luke pushed some branches aside and pointed to the end of a weathered wood dock. "There she—"

He stopped short. Letting the branches swing back, he dashed to the end of the dock.

Joe dropped his duffel bag and pushed past the branches. He heard Wishbone and David race after him across the dock. Joe looked down into the water—and gasped.

A long green canoe lay half submerged. Water had poured in through a dozen large, jagged holes that had been smashed into the bottom of the boat!

RIDDLE OF THE LOST LAKE

by Joanne Barkan

WISHBONE™ created by Rick Duffield

Big Red Chair Books™, *A Division of **Lyrick Publishing***™

This book is a work of fiction. The characters, incidents, and dialogues are products of the author's imagination and are not to be construed as real. Any resemblance to actual events or persons, living or dead, is entirely coincidental.

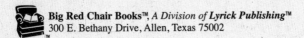 **Big Red Chair Books**™, *A Division of **Lyrick Publishing**™*
300 E. Bethany Drive, Allen, Texas 75002

©2000 Big Feats Entertainment, L.P.

Cover concept and design by Lyle Miller

Interior illustrations by Steven Petruccio

Wishbone photograph by Carol Kaelson

Library of Congress Catalog Card Number: 99-63431

ISBN: 1-57064-540-X

First printing: April 2000

10 9 8 7 6 5 4 3 2 1

Printed in the United States of America

In Memory of
Donald L. Brooks
1956 — 1999
His passion for Squam Lake
inspired many of us

FROM THE BIG RED CHAIR . . .

Oh . . . hi! Wishbone here. You caught me right in the middle of some of my favorite things—books. Let me welcome you to the WISHBONE MYSTERIES. In each story, I help my human friends solve a puzzling mystery. In ***RIDDLE OF THE LOST LAKE***, Joe, David, and I spend part of our summer vacation at Lost Lake looking for an heirloom watch that has been missing for twenty-five years. Once there, we have a second mystery to solve or risk having the lake fall into the hands of greedy developers!

This story takes place in the summer, during the same time period as the second season of my WISHBONE television show. In this story, Joe is fourteen, and he and his friends are going into the ninth grade. Like me, they are always ready for adventure . . . and a good mystery.

You're in for a real treat, so pull up a chair, grab a snack, and sink your teeth into ***RIDDLE OF THE LOST LAKE!***

Chapter One

The freezing rain poured down, and a strong wind was blowing. Raindrops rapped sharply against the window panes of the Talbot house. Wishbone was finishing his lunch in the kitchen. The white Jack Russell terrier with the black patch on his back licked the last bits of food from his dish.

Raising his head, Wishbone said, "Yes! On a stormy Saturday in February, I like a hearty lunch. Then again, I like a hearty lunch *every* day."

Wishbone turned to look at his boy, four-teen-year-old Joe Talbot. Moments earlier, Joe had been eating a turkey sandwich at the kitchen table. But now . . .

"Joe? Joe! Where are you?" Wishbone called out.

No one answered.

Wishbone sighed. "No one ever listens to the dog."

He was about to bark when his sharp ears picked up a sound.

"Footsteps. *Joe's* footsteps. Upstairs, walking along the hallway. Toward the attic!"

With two long leaps, Wishbone bounded out of the kitchen. He raced up the stairs to the second floor. He reached the landing in time to see Joe disappear into the attic.

"Hey, you don't want to go in there without me!" Wishbone called.

He raced after Joe and slipped through the doorway behind him. The rain started falling even harder. It pounded on the roof. It beat against the only window in the attic. Wishbone saw Joe standing among the old furniture and boxes that were piled around. Tall and athletic-looking, Joe had straight brown hair and brown eyes that held a curious expression as he glanced down at a cardboard box that sat on the floor.

Wishbone barked. "The special box!"

Joe turned around. "It's the right kind of day for this, Wishbone."

"Absolutely," Wishbone hurried over to the box and sniffed the lid. "Open it, Joe!"

The big box had belonged to Steve Talbot, Joe's dad. He had died of a rare blood disease when Joe was six years old. Wishbone had heard Joe and his mom, Ellen Talbot, talk about what a fine athlete and an excellent student Steve Talbot had been. Joe's dad had also been a great fan of mystery novels. He'd read them by the dozens and saved his favorites, packing them away in that very box. Wishbone knew Joe shared his father's passion for mystery stories. When Joe first discovered the books in the attic, he promised himself he would read every one.

Joe lifted the lid and took out a stack of books. He sat down on the floor with his back against the heavy box.

"Let's see what we've got today," he murmured. He picked up the first book on the stack. *"Death in a Velvet Jacket* by June Randall," he read out loud.

Wishbone inspected the picture on the cover. "Ugh! There's a cat! I say give it a pass."

Joe picked up the next book. *"The Curse of the No-Hitter* by Robert Appleton."

"Catchy title," Wishbone said. "Put it on the 'possible' pile."

Setting aside the two books, Joe picked up the third one, a small, thin paperback. An old rubber band held it to a thick spiral notebook. When he touched the rubber band, it broke. He read the words on the book's cover.

"Tom Sawyer, Detective by Mark Twain."

Wishbone's ears pricked up. "Mark Twain wrote another book about Tom Sawyer? Ve-e-e-e-ry interesting." He moved closer to check out the book. "Yes! Now I remember. Twain wrote this after *The Adventures of Tom Sawyer* and *Adventures of Huckleberry Finn*. And look, there's a dog on the cover—a handsome bloodhound. Let's go for this one, Joe!"

Joe put down the paperback and opened the old notebook.

Wishbone sighed and stretched out on the floor. "Need I say it again? Nobody ever listens to the dog."

"What a find!" Joe said a moment later. He stared at the notebook in amazement. "This is my dad's journal! He wrote it the summer he was fourteen."

Wishbone jumped up and sniffed the notebook.

"This is about his life," Joe said. He ran his hand over the worn cardboard cover.

Wishbone studied the expression on Joe's face. He could guess what his friend was feeling. *Reading the notebook will be like hearing your dad talk—or even think. You'll find out so much about him, Joe.*

Joe turned the notebook over. As he did, something fell out of it. It was an old photograph. As Joe picked it up from the dusty floor, Wishbone studied the picture.

"There's my dad on the left," Joe said.

Wishbone gazed at a tanned, athletic-looking boy with a grin similar to Joe's. His eyes were slightly lighter than Joe's. His straight brown hair was a bit darker. Like the three other young people in the photograph, he wore his hair long. A red bandana was tied around his forehead.

"That's Steve, all right," Wishbone said, wagging his tail. He had seen many photos of Joe's dad. "Who are the others, Joe? And where are they?"

The picture showed Steve sitting on a wooden dock with three other teenagers. The dock stretched out over dark, still water. In back of them was nothing but woods.

The energetic-looking boy kneeling next to Steve Talbot had wavy blond hair and a playful smile. He wore wire-rimmed glasses. Next to him sat a girl with dark hair down to her waist. She wore an Indian print blouse and was reading a book that she held quite close to her face. On the far right sat a muscular boy who looked a few years older. His large, green eyes stared straight into the camera. A bandana held back his wild black hair.

Joe turned the photograph over. "Here's a date," he murmured. "It's the same summer as the journal. And four names. Steve Talbot, Luke Talbot, Tina Tucker, and John 'Mac' MacKenzie."

Joe breathed in sharply. He pointed at some words written across the bottom of the photo in red ink.

"This is my dad's handwriting. Look what he wrote, Wishbone!" Joe said.

Wishbone stared at the words as Joe read them aloud.

LOST LAKE—SCENE OF AN UNSOLVED CRIME.

Chapter Two

Joe couldn't stop staring at the words. "Scene of an unsolved crime? What crime? What did it have to do with my dad? And what's Lost Lake?"

Wishbone sniffed the photo. To Joe, he seemed equally curious.

"There's only one way to find out more," Joe said.

He tucked the photo into the middle of the notebook and turned to the first page his dad had written. Joe began to read out loud. Wishbone settled down with his head in Joe's lap. As Joe read, real time seemed to fade away. In his mind, the people and places in the journal took shape like scenes in a movie. Joe imagined what it was like when his father was fourteen.

July 1. Got to Lost Lake this afternoon. Gram and Pops Talbot and Luke were waiting for me at the

**bus stop in Woodwich. The instant I stepped off
the bus, I could smell the pines and feel the spirit
of the lake all around me . . .**

"Just look at you, Steve," Gram Talbot said. "You must have grown six inches this past year. What do they feed you at home?"

"Whatever it is, it makes his hair grow, too," Pops said.

Steve Talbot gave his grandmother and grandfather a hug. They hadn't changed at all since the previous summer. As usual, they both wore hiking pants, sneakers, and T-shirts. Gram's salt-and-pepper hair was cut short. Her camera hung from a strap around her neck. A beat-up sailor's cap covered Pops's unruly white hair.

Steve grinned as he shook hands with Luke Talbot, his first cousin. Although their families lived a thousand miles apart, they were the best of friends. Luke was just two months older than Steve. Since they were toddlers, they had spent every summer on Lost Lake with their grandparents. Although Gram and Pops looked the same, Luke had changed. He was almost as tall as Steve. He wore his hair longer than the summer before. And there was something else. Behind his wire-rimmed glasses, his gray eyes weren't twinkling with laughter the way they usually were.

"I have to talk to you about something later," he murmured to Steve. Then his expression changed. He jabbed his cousin's shoulder playfully. "I've been here for two days, Talbot. You know what that means. I've had two days of hiking and swimming. Let's face it—you'll never catch up."

Steve hoisted his duffel bag onto one shoulder. "Don't bet on it, Talbot," he said to Luke, "As soon as we get to our own dock, I'll race you across the cove. Front crawl all the way. You don't stand a chance."

Luke sighed and shook his head. "Always the dreamer."

Gram, Pops, Steve, and Luke walked across the center of Woodwich. Large trees shaded the white, two-story buildings on the tiny town square. The buildings housed a post office, a sheriff's office, a half-dozen shops, and a snack bar. On the far side of the square was the town dock. Woodwich sat on the edge of Lost Lake.

As they approached the dock, Steve's eyes were fixed on the clear, deep water. Sunlight skipped across the surface. Along the edge of the lake the water reflected the dark greens of the surrounding woods. Beyond the woods rose a line of tree-covered mountains.

Steve looked for the five huge boulders that rose out of the water, far beyond the dock. They were souvenirs of the last Ice Age. Some thirty thousand years earlier, a glacier had carved a deep basin out of the land. This became Lost Lake. The glacier left hundreds of gigantic boulders scattered across the lake bottom.

Steve breathed in deeply. He wanted to take in everything—the fresh air, the blue sky, the mountains, and the jewel-like lake.

"Lost Lake's lookin' good," Luke said.

Steve nodded. He knew Luke felt the same way he did about the lake. They loved being there more than anyplace else.

The two Talbot canoes were tied to the dock. Steve and Luke put the duffel bag into one canoe. They took off their sneakers and tossed them next to the bag. Then they untied the rope and hopped in. Steve sat in front Luke in back. They dipped their wood paddles into the water, and the aluminum canoe slid away from the dock. Two more strokes, and they were gliding across the satinlike surface. Just behind them, Gram and Pops paddled the second canoe.

Steve felt the rhythm in his arms and shoulders: stroke, glide, stroke, glide.

Like the Penacook Indians, he thought.

The Penacooks had lived in the area around Lost Lake some six hundred years earlier. Steve imagined himself as a tribal hunter, paddling his birch-bark canoe across the lake, heading for the five boulders. Europeans didn't arrive until much later. The first were French trappers in the seventeenth century. Upon returning home, the trappers had described the amazingly beautiful lake to their friends. But no one was able to find it again for several years. For that reason, it was named Lost Lake.

Beyond the five boulders lay the largest and most open part of Lost Lake. Everyone called it the main lake. Only a few small, tree-covered islands broke the expanse of water. Beyond the main lake lay Moose Cove, where the Talbots had their summer place.

"What did you want to tell me?" Steve asked.

"It's about Tina Tucker," Luke answered.

Tina was a good friend of the Talbot cousins. Her family lived on the lake all year. They owned the property next to the Talbots'.

"She hinted at something about leaving the lake," Luke continued. "I asked her about it, but she wouldn't say anything else. She said she couldn't."

Steve was still thinking about this when the canoe reached the five boulders. The boys headed for the narrow passage between the two largest boulders. Other huge rocks lay just beneath the surface. People who didn't know the lake well often scraped their canoes against the rocks or broke their paddles. Luke and Steve liked to paddle through the passage with their eyes closed. They considered it proof of how well they knew the lake.

"Time for a little shut-eye," Steve said to Luke.

Both boys closed their eyes. In his mind, Steve saw the pattern of rocks shimmering underwater. A minute or so later, they had cleared the boulders without so much as a bump.

"An extraordinary steering job," Luke said. Sitting in the back of the canoe, he did the steering. "Sometimes I amaze myself."

In response, Steve flicked his paddle so that water splashed over Luke's knees.

"Hey! That's a declaration of war," Luke said.

He flicked his own paddle so that water splashed over Steve's head. By the time the canoes entered Moose Cove, both boys were half-soaked.

On the far shore, Steve could see the three family camps he knew so well. All the properties on Lost Lake were called "camps." Each camp was a series of small cabins tucked away in the woods.

The Talbot camp was on the left. It consisted of three buildings. There was the main cabin where his grandparents lived. A smaller one-room cabin had two beds where Steve and Luke slept. There was also a woodshed. The chimney of the main cabin was just visible through the trees. An ancestor, Josiah Talbot, had built the cabin himself in the nineteenth century.

To the right of the Talbot camp was the Tucker family camp. To the right of the Tuckers' camp was the MacKenzies'. Each camp had a small wooden dock.

Steve noticed someone sitting on the Talbot dock, reading. He recognized the very long, dark hair.

"Tina Tucker!" Steve said. He raised his paddle straight up. "Hey, Tuck!"

The girl on the dock stood up and waved. At that moment, someone else emerged from the woods and stepped onto the dock. He looked about seventeen years old. His wild black hair was held back by a bandana.

"Mac!" Steve shouted, raising his paddle a second time.

As the two canoes approached the dock, Luke called out, "Who's racing across the cove with us?"

"I'm in," Tina called back. She smiled, but it seemed strained. Steve wondered again about what Luke had told him. Was it possible her family really *was* leaving Lost Lake?

"Not me." Mac's answer cut into Steve's thought. "I just came to say hi."

"Mac's not doing anything this summer unless it brings in big money," Luke told Steve. "All work and no play. That's a big mistake, Mac."

"Hey, if I don't work I'll never earn money for my cross-country trip," Mac said. He glanced at his watch. He, too, looked different to Steve, more serious.

"Wait a minute," Gram said as she and Pops steadied their canoe next to the dock. "Nobody goes anywhere until I get a picture. First photo of the season. Let's have all of you on the dock."

Steve and Luke paddled to the far side of the dock and scrambled out of their canoe. After Luke tied the canoe, the four friends arranged themselves in a row. As Gram looked through the camera's viewfinder, Steve noticed the thin paperback book in Tina's hand. He read the words on the cover.

"*Tom Sawyer, Detective* by Mark Twain. How is it?" he asked.

"Groovy," Tina said. She opened the book, looking at it closely. "You've got to read it when I'm finished."

Steve turned toward the camera and grinned. It was summer vacation. He was back at Lost Lake. Nothing could go wrong.

Click.

Joe stopped reading the journal.

"My dad crossed out the last sentence on

this page. It looks like the same red pen he used to write on the back of the photo."

Joe stared at the words.

~~Nothing could go wrong.~~

"What happened that summer?" he wondered out loud.

He opened the paperback copy of *Tom Sawyer, Detective*. There was something written on the inside of the front cover:

This book belongs to Tina Tucker.

"This must be the book in the photograph," Joe said.

He jumped up and stacked the other books back in the box. Then he hurried to the attic door, carrying his dad's journal and *Tom Sawyer, Detective*.

"Maybe Mom knows something about this," he said. "Come on, Wishbone."

Wishbone stood up and shook himself. His nails clicked on the wood floor as he trotted after Joe.

Downstairs, Joe found his mom working at the computer in the study. She was wearing jeans and a sweater. She looked up with a smile when Joe rushed into the room.

"What's up?" she asked, tucking her brown, shoulder-length hair behind her ears.

"Major discovery," Joe said. He sat down on

the sofa. Wishbone jumped up and sat next to Joe. "I found the journal Dad kept the summer he was fourteen. There was an old photo in it." Joe handed both to his mother. "They were in Dad's special box."

Ellen studied the photograph first. She smiled, but her eyes looked sad as well."I've never seen this one before," she said. She opened the notebook. As she flipped through it, a thoughtful expression came into her eyes. After a few minutes, she closed the journal and moved to the sofa to sit next to Joe.

"I'm so happy you found this. You'll learn a lot about your dad." She turned the notebook over in her hands. "I'd like to read it, too."

"Something really weird happened that summer," Joe said. "Look at this."

He showed his mother the words on the back of the photo and the crossed-out sentence in the journal. "What do you know about Lost Lake?" he asked. "Did you ever go there?"

Ellen shook her head. "I never saw the lake. It's up in New England. Your dad and I planned to take you there some day. He called it his favorite place in the world."

As Joe stared at the photo, he wanted to know more about his dad, the Talbot's and the place that had been so special to them.

"Did you know Luke Talbot?" he asked his mom.

"I met him the weekend of our wedding," she replied. "He was our best man. We all loved being with him. He was a great guitar player and singer. I'm sure he still is," she added. "He mentioned in one of his holiday cards that he's teaching music in Boston. I'm sorry he lives so far away. It's been many, many years since I've seen him."

"Does he still spend summers on Lost Lake?" Joe asked.

His mother nodded. "He loved the lake as much as your father did. He inherited the Talbot place after their grandparents died."

Ellen leafed through a few more pages of the journal. Something caught her eye, and she starting reading carefully.

"Yes! Now I remember," she said. "Your father told me about that summer." She looked up at Joe. "The Talbot family's gold-and-diamond heirloom watch was stolen."

Joe eyes opened wide in surprise. "I never heard about an heirloom watch," he said. "It was stolen?"

"Yes," his mother answered. "It was pretty terrible for your dad and for Luke. They blamed themselves."

Chapter Three

"**A** stolen heirloom!" Wishbone lifted his head to sniff Steve Talbot's journal. "Wow, the Talbots have a family mystery. Luckily they also have a family detective—me."

"Did anyone ever find the watch?" Joe asked.

"No," Ellen said. "As far as your father knew, it was an unsolved mystery." She handed the journal back to Joe. "You'll probably find details about what happened in here. And remember, as soon as you finish reading, it's my turn."

Wishbone scrambled off the sofa as Joe stood up.

"I'd like to try solving the mystery. Want to help, Wishbone?" Joe asked.

"You bet I do!" Wishbone said. He followed Joe out of the study. "How about a quick snack break first, Joe? . . . Joe? Oh, well, can't win 'em all."

Upstairs, in the bedroom they shared, Joe and Wishbone stretched out on the bed. Joe opened the notebook.

"I've got to find the first time my dad mentions the stolen watch," Joe said. He searched through the journal for several minutes. "Got it!"

He began to read out loud.

July 31. I wish I could live this day over again. I'd make it come out a different way. The Talbot watch is gone! What makes it worse, much worse—it's Luke's and my fault!

"This watch is so hip," Steve said to Luke.

It was late afternoon. The cousins stood next to the old desk in their grandparents' small bedroom in the main cabin. In the palm of Steve's hand lay a solid-gold pocket watch—the Talbot family heirloom. It had been crafted during the 1860s. Two fine diamonds sparkled on the cover. Between them, the watchmaker had engraved a large, fancy "T."

Gram and Pops kept the watch locked in a drawer in the desk. But Luke and Steve were allowed to take it out and look at it.

Steve opened the watch and read the inscription on the inside of the cover.

"Josiah Howell Talbot. Twelfth Regiment, Union Army."

Both boys knew the stories about Josiah Talbot by heart. Josiah had fought bravely during the Civil War as a young man. Lying wounded in an army hospital, he had shaken hands with President Abraham Lincoln. Many years after the war, he had bought the property on Lost Lake.

"A first-class family hero," Luke said. "Maybe someday one of us will name a kid after him. Josiah . . . Joseph . . . How about Joe? Joe Talbot."

"I'd definitely—"

A shout interrupted Steve. It came from the direction of the dock.

"Attention, all you landlubbers!" a voice called out. "I've got the fish of the century here!"

"It's Pops!" Steve said. "He's caught a big one!"

Steve placed the watch on the desktop. The two boys dashed out of the cabin and raced down the path to the dock. They had almost reached it when Luke stopped short.

"Gram will definitely want a picture," he said. "I saw her camera in the cabin, on the big table. I'll go back and get it."

As Luke jogged back to the cabin, Steve went on to the dock. Pops was unloading his fishing gear from the canoe. He saw Steve and held up a large bass with a greenish back and silvery sides.

"Right on, Pops!" Steve shouted. "That's a beauty. It must be four pounds."

"At least!" Pops said with a laugh. He looked around. "Where is everyone? I want to show this off."

Steve reached into the canoe for the last of the fishing gear. "Luke's getting the camera," he said. "And Gram is still over at the Tucker camp, helping them pack."

Thinking of Tina, he shook his head sadly. He could hardly believe she was moving away from Lost Lake. But she was. Her family was leaving the next morning. And Steve still didn't know why. Whenever he'd asked, Tina just said they had to. It was clear the subject pained her. So Steve had stopped asking.

He turned to see Luke running up to the dock. He was carrying Gram's camera.

"Let's get this historic moment on film," Luke said. "Hold that bass high and smile for future generations."

Pops stood with one arm around Steve and the other raised to show the fish. Just as Luke was about to snap the picture, Mac MacKenzie appeared.

"What's happening, man?" he asked. "I heard someone shouting about a fish."

"Get in the picture," Luke said, waving him toward Steve and Pops.

Mac joined the pair at the end of the dock. "This is one weird family. Every time I show up, I get my picture taken."

"Hey, we Talbots care about preserving our family history," Luke said. He snapped the picture.

Mac checked his watch. "Gotta go to work," he said.

He was *always* saying that, Steve noticed. It seemed all Mac thought about these days was money and his cross-country trip.

Steve glanced at Luke as something else occurred to him. "We left the Talbot watch out," he said.

Luke turned toward the cabin, but Steve ran past him.

"I'll put it away," he said.

When he got to the cabin, Steve hurried up the porch steps. He walked through the main room to the small hallway that led to the bedroom. In three steps he had crossed the room to the desk and reached for the watch.

It was gone!

Steve's heart started racing. He pushed aside papers, pencils, postage stamps, envelopes— everything on the desktop. No watch. He dropped down to his knees and searched the floor near the desk. He felt around the wood boards with his hands.

Where could it be? he asked himself again and again.

He stood up and searched through every drawer in the desk. Nothing. He looked under the bed, under the night tables, under the cushion on the window seat.

He moaned out loud. "This isn't really happening," he moaned. "It can't be!" He took a deep breath. "Okay, Talbot, calm down and search slowly."

The minutes slipped by. Steve went over every inch of the desk. He heard Pops and Luke talking as they walked up to the cabin. The screen door opened and shut. A moment later, Luke was standing in the bedroom doorway.

"You're still here?" he asked. "What've you been doing?"

Steve stared at Luke. He knew his voice was going to shake when he spoke. He breathed in.

"The Talbot watch is gone. It's vanished!"

After dinner that evening, Steve and Luke sat on the front porch of the cabin.

"I wish I could live this day over again," Steve said. "I'd never leave the watch out. I'd lock it right back in the drawer—just the way we always did."

"It's a bummer," Luke said. "Like a bad dream, only you can't wake up."

29

"I know Gram and Pops are trying not to make us feel worse than we already do," Steve said. "But they're both upset."

Luke nodded. "You can see it in their eyes."

"Maybe the watch is still in the cabin somewhere," Steve said. He sighed. "But we spent three hours searching the place. And no one is better at finding things than Gram."

"There *is* another alternative," Luke pointed out.

Steve hesitated. He, too, had thought of another possibility. "You mean that someone stole the watch."

"Yep," Luke said.

Steve pushed back his long hair. "Okay, let's take this step by step. Say someone *did* take the watch. It had to happen between the time we left the watch on the desk and the time I told you it was missing. The way I see it, only three people were in or near the cabin during that time."

"Right," Luke said. "I'm one of them. I was in the cabin alone when I got the camera and loaded it with film."

"I'm another," Steve went on. "I was in the bedroom looking for the watch for about ten minutes before you and Pops got back."

The boys fell silent until Luke said, "We both know who the third person is."

Steve nodded. "Mac MacKenzie. The path

from the MacKenzie camp to our dock goes right by this cabin."

Wishbone sat up when Joe stopped reading. Joe put down his dad's journal and folded one arm behind his head. "Could I have solved the mystery if I had been at Lost Lake that summer?" he wondered aloud. "Probably not. Not if my dad couldn't." He rubbed Wishbone's head with his other hand. "But you never know. Maybe I would have noticed something. Just one clue."

Wishbone sighed happily. "Joe, someone with a head-rubbing technique like yours could do *anything.*"

"I wish I had a lake to go to every summer with my best friends," Joe continued. "And a cabin. And lots of canoeing and hiking and swimming races. I wish I could see Lost Lake . . . and meet my dad's cousin Luke."

A moment later, Wishbone scrambled aside as Joe sat straight up. "Maybe I can!" he exclaimed. "Maybe I can write to Luke Talbot and ask to visit Lost Lake this summer. If I work at the bookstore a few hours every week and save all my money, I could pay for the trip."

The words rushed out of Joe's mouth. Then he became thoughtful. "Suppose I can get to Lost

Lake. Maybe I can figure out what happened to the Talbot heirloom watch."

"Don't forget the part about taking along the dog," Wishbone said. "Joe? Are you listening, Joe?"

Chapter Four

Wishbone stood on the bus seat and pressed his nose against the glass of the large window.

"We're really doing it, Joe! We're on our way to Lost Lake! The view from here sure is better than the one from the airplane baggage compartment. Boy, am I glad to be out of there!"

Five months had passed. It was a Tuesday afternoon in early July. Joe had earned enough money for a week-long trip to Lost Lake for himself and Wishbone. Joe had invited David Barnes, one of his best friends from home in Oakdale, to come along. They had traveled by plane to an airport that was three hours from the town of Woodwich. They were completing the trip by bus.

Wishbone turned away from the tree-covered mountains to look at his friends. Joe and David sat across the aisle. They seemed completely focused on the laptop computer in front of David.

"I've already started keeping a complete electronic file on the case," David said. He had short, dark curly hair and light-brown skin. He was good at figuring out almost anything.

"Business before pleasure," Wishbone reminded himself. "This is going to be a working vacation for the dog." He jumped to the floor and started to climb onto his friends' seats. Joe helped him up. "How about filling in the canine member of the detective team?"

"Check this out," David said to Joe. His fingers moved nimbly across the computer's keyboard. A file name appeared on the screen. Joe read it out loud.

```
CASE: MISSING TALBOT WATCH.
STATUS: UNSOLVED.
```

David's intense, dark eyes shone with excitement as he opened several windows on the screen.

"I've set up a separate window for each category," he said. "Basic facts, suspects, clues, interviews . . ."

Wishbone sniffed the computer. "Excellent work, David. Now all you need is a Wishbone window for must-know information. That includes my tips on mystery-solving and my snack schedule."

Joe was studying the computer screen. "Let's go over suspects again. Both my dad and Luke had an opportunity to take the watch— but no reason to take it. We need a motive."

"What about the guy named Mac MacKenzie?" David asked. "You said you found out more about him in your dad's journal."

"*We* found out more," Wishbone said. "Let's keep the record straight."

"Listen to this," Joe said. He opened the journal and started reading.

August 23. Everyone went over to the MacKenzie camp this morning to say good-bye to Mac.

"That's quite a vehicle you've got," Gram said to Mac.

"Out of sight, man," Steve said.

A dozen friends had gathered with Mac's family in the clearing behind the MacKenzie cabin. Next to the family's brown station wagon stood an iridescent blue Volkswagen bus. Red, yellow, and pink letters along one side spelled out *BORN TO DRIVE*. Along the other side ran the words *CALIFORNIA DREAMER*. A large white dove wearing a pair of sunglasses was painted on the hood.

"Are you the artist?" Pops asked Mac.

"Nope," Mac said. He was wearing bell-bottomed jeans, a red T-shirt, a purple fringed vest, and an old cowboy hat. "The guy who sold me the bus did the paint job. Fantastic, isn't it?"

"What's *under* the paint job is more important," Mrs. MacKenzie murmured. "I hope it's in good condition."

"Don't worry, Mom," Mac said. "The auto shop in Woodwich checked everything out. Well, fans, gotta split."

Mac looked as if he were itching to be on the road. He said his good-byes. Then he opened the bus door and climbed onto the driver's seat.

"I don't know how he managed to save enough money to buy that bus so quickly," Mr. MacKenzie said as the motor rumbled once and settled into a steady purr. "I guess he just wanted it badly enough."

Luke frowned. "Badly enough to steal the Talbot family watch?" he whispered to Steve.

Mac waved as he started down the narrow dirt driveway to begin his cross-country trip.

"Bon voyage!" Pops called out.

"Catch you later, man," Steve shouted.

He and Luke walked back to the Talbot camp together.

"Do you really think Mac could have stolen the watch?" Steve asked. "He's our friend, not a thief. He seemed pretty shocked when we told him it was missing."

"I know. I don't want to think he did it, either," Luke said. "It's just that he's been so totally obsessed this summer. All he talked about was earning money for that bus and the trip."

"True," Steve said. "But maybe something else happened to the watch. Something totally weird, totally unexpected. We've just got to discover the first clue."

"Watch out, folks," Luke said with a laugh. "The youth sleuth of Lost Lake is at it again." His smile faded. "Seriously, Talbot, keep reading those mystery novels. If you come up with another explanation for the missing watch, I'll go for it. I hate thinking that Mac stole anything."

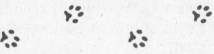

"Let me get this into the computer," David said. Again his fingers danced across the keys. "Mac buys VW bus. Gets the money very quickly. Too quickly?" He closed the window for suspects. "What's next, Joe?"

Joe didn't answer. He was examining something in his dad's copy of *Tom Sawyer, Detective*.

"I never noticed this before," he said. "Two pages at the end of the book are stuck together."

David peered over Joe's shoulder. "They're just advertising for other books," he said, shrugging.

"That's why I never paid attention to them before," Joe said. "Still . . ."

He carefully slipped the edge of his fingernail between the two pages and worked at the stuck parts until the two pages separated.

"Hey, look at this," Joe said. "One of the pages didn't have anything printed on it. So someone used it to write on." He studied the page for a moment. Then he showed David the faded writing in pencil. "It's my dad's handwriting—only really small."

Joe held the book closer to the window to get more light. His eyes skimmed over the page.

"It's a list," he said, growing more excited. "A list of links between *Tom Sawyer, Detective* and the missing watch on Lost Lake. It's all the things my dad noticed when he read the book."

David's eyes shone as he looked over Joe's shoulder. "Cool."

"This must be why my dad kept the book and his journal together," Joe said. "There was a rubber band around them both when I found them." He looked up at David. "Can you make a new window for this list?"

"Sure." David turned back to the computer and began working. He set up the window and an icon for it. "Tell me what you've got."

"Okay. Here's what my dad wrote," Joe said. He squinted at the small-sized writing, reading out loud.

"'Tom Sawyer and his good friend Huck Finn return to a place they like a lot for summer vacation. Steve and Luke Talbot return to Lost Lake for the summer.'"

David typed for a minute. "Got it."

Joe continued. "'Tom and Huck visit Tom's Uncle Silas and his family on their farm. They expect it to be as peaceful and friendly as usual, but it's not. Two thieves who've stolen two diamonds kill someone and bury him nearby. The body is so badly beaten that no one can identify it. Everyone thinks the dead man is a neighbor, Jubiter Dunlap. Even though Uncle Silas was well-liked in the town, people turned against him. They blamed him for the murder. He actually feels responsible for it even though he's not guilty.'"

David continued typing. When he finished, Joe read the links to the watch mystery.

"'Steve and Luke expect a peaceful summer at Lost Lake, as usual. But a crime takes place. A watch with two diamonds is stolen. A friend, Mac MacKenzie, might be involved. Steve and Luke feel responsible for the missing watch even though they're not guilty.'"

Joe frowned. "The links are pretty cool. But none of it seems very useful for solving the watch mystery."

"You never know," David said. He finished typing, then hit the keys to save the information. "Maybe this will come in handy later."

Joe flipped through the pages of the paperback. "Remember Tom Sawyer's method of observing people? He used it to figure out that a stranger who seemed to be deaf was really Jubiter Dunlap in disguise. That's how he figured out that Jubiter wasn't murdered after all."

David nodded. "Tom Sawyer always noticed the gestures people made when they were worried or feeling guilty. Some rubbed their chins. Others kept tapping a cheek. They'd do it without even realizing it."

"Right," Joe said. "I'm going to watch people and look for nervous habits while we're at Lost Lake."

David laughed. "If you're Tom Sawyer, I guess that makes me Huck Finn." He scrolled slowly through the computer file. "Hey, I just realized something. This case file includes three pairs of friends. Your dad and Luke, Tom and Huck, and you and me."

Wishbone barked sharply from the seat across the aisle. "And you, too, Wishbone," Joe said.

"Woodwich," the bus driver called out. "Two minutes to the Woodwich bus stop."

Joe's heart beat faster. *This is it,* he thought. *I'm about to see everything my dad described. I'm about to live it!*

The bus slowed down as it approached the

town. Joe noticed more houses along the road. They passed a sign.

Woodwich
Population: 1,432

After a right turn, the bus passed a few stores housed in wood-framed buildings painted white. It pulled up alongside a bench shaded by a simple wood awning. The words *Bus Stop* were painted on the back of the bench. When the driver turned off the motor, Joe began dragging his duffel bag to the front of the bus. David and Wishbone followed close behind him. The door opened. As Joe stepped down from the bus, he glanced at the half-dozen people waiting near the bench. His eyes were immediately drawn to one of them.

That's him, Joe thought. *That's Luke Talbot.*

Joe nodded at the energetic-looking man with wavy blond hair that was graying at the temples. He wore wire-rimmed glasses, a T-shirt, faded Bermuda shorts, and no shoes. He waved at Joe. A smile tilted up at one corner of his mouth.

"Joe Talbot," the man said as he shook Joe's hand. "I'd know you anywhere." He studied Joe's face but didn't say anything else for a moment. Joe knew he was thinking about Steve Talbot.

Turning to David, the man said, "I'm Luke Talbot. I suppose you've already guessed that. You must be David Barnes. Welcome to Lost Lake. I'm really pleased to have you and Joe here."

"Nice to meet you," David said.

Luke's smile broadened as he glanced down at Wishbone. "This good-looking fellow must be Wishbone," he said. "I'm sure he'll be an excellent addition to the Talbot camp. We need a dog."

Joe felt Wishbone's wagging tail thump against his leg. "I think he likes it here already," Joe said.

As Luke led the way across the town square, Joe took everything in: the crisp, pine-scented air; the white, wood-framed buildings; the shade trees; and the wide, blue waters of Lost Lake, stretching into the distance.

"Wow, Woodwich looks just the way my dad described it in his journal," he said.

Luke nodded. "This place hasn't changed much over the years. I just hope you won't end up disappointed if you can't solve the mystery of the Talbot watch. After more than twenty-five years, I'm afraid not even Sherlock Holmes would get very far." He shrugged and smiled at the boys. "But who knows? You two could be even better than the great Holmes."

At the town dock, Joe saw a dozen people getting in and out of canoes, rowboats, and motorboats. Beyond the dock the town seemed to end and woods began. Luke turned left and walked along a dirt path under tall trees.

"I always leave my canoe at a little dock that's tucked away in the woods," he explained to Joe and David. "It's quicker because almost no one uses it. So get ready to see my pride and joy."

"Your canoe?" Joe asked.

"Yes, indeed," Luke said. "A new, twelve-foot, fiberglass model by ClassCraft. There's no

finer canoe made today. It took a chunk of my savings to pay for it. But my old one gave out completely."

Luke pushed some branches aside and pointed to the end of a weathered wood dock. "There she—"

He stopped short. Letting the branches swing back, he dashed to the end of the dock. Joe dropped his duffel bag and pushed past the branches. He heard Wishbone and David race after him, along the dock. Joe looked down into the water—and gasped.

A long green canoe lay half submerged. Water had poured in through a dozen large, jagged holes that had been smashed through the bottom of the boat!

Chapter Five

Standing on the dock, Wishbone leaned over his front paws and looked at the wrecked canoe. "Yikes!"

"Someone took an axe to it," Luke said. His gray eyes were round with disbelief. "It's totally destroyed." He raked his hands through his hair. "This is the second time I've lost something of value on the lake!"

"The first was the Talbot watch," Joe said.

"That's right." Luke took a deep breath. "We've got to report this to the sheriff."

Wishbone scratched his left ear. "Hmm, missing watch and smashed canoe. Looks like I've got two mysteries to solve!"

He shook himself from head to tail and pricked up his ears. "Stand aside, folks. Make way for Super Sleuth!"

Wishbone and his friends hurried back to the town square. One of the small white buildings was the sheriff's office. Inside they found a heavy-set, gray-haired man with a gray moustache sitting behind a tidy desk. He was about fifty-five years old and wore khaki slacks and a matching shirt. A star-shaped pin was fastened to his shirt pocket. He stood up as soon as he saw them.

"Hey there, Luke," he said. "Are these the visitors you were telling me about last week?"

"That's right," Luke told him.

The sheriff shook hands with both boys and rubbed Wishbone's head. "You must be Steve Talbot's son," he said to Joe. "I'm Bill Eastwood. I was born and raised in Woodwich. So I've known your family for more than a half-century."

"I wish this were just a social visit, Bill," Luke said. "But I have a problem."

Wishbone listened carefully while Luke explained what had happened to his canoe. The sheriff's face grew more and more serious. He sat down and began writing up a report.

"When did you leave the canoe at the dock?" he asked.

"About two hours ago," Luke said. "I was doing errands in town."

"Any ideas about who would have done this?" the sheriff asked.

"Not a one," Luke replied.

"Who knows that you leave your canoe at the little dock?" the sheriff went on.

"All my friends and neighbors."

The sheriff looked up. "There's a chance that an outsider could have done this. Some crazy prankster just passing through or here for a day of fishing. But it doesn't seem likely." He glanced at Joe and David. "That kind of vandalism almost never happens in Woodwich."

He stood up and said to Luke, "I'll go and take a good look at the canoe. My deputy can haul it out of the water. I'd like to keep it in our back lot for now. I'll ask around town and find out whatever I can. In the meantime, you can borrow my canoe to get home. It's tied up at the town dock. Use it as long as you need it."

Wishbone barked in agreement when Luke, Joe, and David thanked the sheriff. Then they all left the building together. Wishbone followed his friends across the square toward the lake. He couldn't help noticing that Luke walked with his hands stuffed deep in his pockets.

"Well, if anyone can dig up information about the canoe, Bill Eastwood can." Luke said. "He knows everything about everyone in town."

"Yo, Talbot!" A shout came from across the street.

Wishbone turned to see three people standing in front of a small grocery store. Luke nodded when he saw them.

"Come on, guys," he said to Joe and David. "I want you to meet these people."

As they crossed the street, Wishbone noticed that Joe watched the three people closely. "Practicing Tom Sawyer's method of observing, eh? Good work, Joe!"

The first person Wishbone saw was a man, shorter than Luke but more muscular. His wild black hair was streaked with gray. His large green eyes stared straight at Joe. Next to him stood a woman with short red hair and a friendly smile. The third person was a teenage boy, about eighteen. He was leaning against a large BMW motorcycle. He balanced a helmet with one hand on the long, sleek seat. He was muscular like the man and red-haired like the woman. He wore black jeans, leather boots, and a sleeveless T-shirt.

Hmm, Wishbone thought. *That man, the one who's having a bad hair day . . . I know him from somewhere.*

"Meet the MacKenzie family," Luke said. "This is Mac, his wife, Linda, and their son, Pat. They're our neighbors on Moose Cove. Their daughter Kelly is at a school camp this summer."

"Mac! Of course!" Wishbone said. "From the photograph!"

Mac's eyes remained fixed on Joe. He stepped forward and held out his hand.

"You're Steve Talbot's son," he said a little hesitantly. "I heard you were coming. Nice to meet you."

Luke introduced David. After everyone shook hands, there was a moment of awkward silence. Wishbone sniffed the air. "Why isn't anybody talking?"

"Awesome bike," David finally said to Pat. He stepped closer to examine the controls.

"I'll say!" Joe ran one hand lightly over a sleek panel. Silver flecks in the dark red paint made the color shimmer.

"Isn't she a beauty?" Pat said.

"It'll take Pat five summers to pay off the loan," Mac said. "But he's making a good start. He's doing yard work and carpentry for several families on the lake."

"Lots of tree-trimming and deck-building," Pat said. "But it's worth it."

There was another silence. Wishbone looked from Mac to Luke. The two men looked uneasy.

"Well, I want to show these fellows around the Talbot camp before the sun goes down," Luke said finally. "We'll see you folks around Moose Cove."

Wishbone trotted alongside Joe to the town dock.

"You and Mac seem sort of . . . " Joe began.

Luke nodded. "I know what you mean.

We're not unfriendly, really. But we're not close friends anymore. Mac guessed that Steve and I suspected him of taking the Talbot watch. I tried to tell him years ago that I didn't believe he had anything to do with it. But he's always been distant toward me."

"So you don't believe he took the watch?" David asked.

Luke shrugged. "It's been so long. I don't *think* he did. Maybe I just don't *want* to believe it. What happened is still a complete mystery. In any case, it wasn't worth a friendship. I'm sorry the watch changed things between us."

They found the sheriff's canoe and climbed into it. Wishbone settled in the middle of the canoe, next to David. Luke took up a paddle in back, while Joe took another in front. As Luke pushed the boat away from the dock, Wishbone shifted his weight from paw to paw to keep his balance.

"Let's forget about missing watches and wrecked canoes for now," Luke said. "You boys deserve a proper introduction to Lost Lake."

"I hope that includes food." Wishbone looked out over the water. "Does anybody remember the word *snack?*"

There were five huge boulders in the distance. Wishbone saw that Joe and David had noticed them, too.

"Do you still paddle between those rocks

with your eyes closed?" David asked. "We read about that in Joe's dad's journal."

Luke laughed. "I admit, I still try it now and again. Good grief, Steve must have put everything in that journal!"

Minutes later, they glided past the boulders and into the main part of the lake. Joe stopped paddling long enough to dip his hand into the water. "Pretty cold," he said, shivering. Wishbone saw the way his boy's eyes followed the wooded sweep of the shoreline. It was broken only here and there by a small dock. The surrounding mountains reflected the warm glow of the late afternoon sun.

"It all looks just the way I imagined it would," Joe said.

David nodded. "I was thinking the same thing."

O-o-o-o-o-o-o-o-a! O-o-o-o-o-o-a!

An eerie but spellbinding call echoed across the lake.

Wishbone stood tall, with his neck stretched out and his muzzle pointing up. "That's not on my list of known sounds," he said. His whole body trembled, on the alert.

Luke's voice was soothing. "It's okay, Wishbone. It's a loon. Their calls often spook dogs."

"Spooked?" Wishbone blinked. "I'm not spooked. Just sniffing out the territory."

"My dad wrote about the loons," Joe said.

"He made them sound pretty amazing."

"They're the most treasured creatures on the lake," Luke said. "A half-century ago, the loon population had dropped down to just six. The Loon Protection Society began a campaign to get people to respect the birds' habitat. Now we've got thirteen pair on the lake and five nests this summer. If you've never seen a loon, you're in for a treat."

They continued paddling. About ten minutes later, Luke pointed suddenly to the right. "Look! A loon just surfaced from a dive."

About twenty yards away, a large, strikingly beautiful bird was bobbing on the water. It had a jet black head and a long, pointed black bill. A band of black-and-white stripes formed a ring around its black neck. Just below, a patch of snow white was visible above the water. The rest of the bird—its back, wings, and tail—were covered with a bold black-and-white pattern of stripes, squares, and dots.

"Wow," David said. "It's really cool-looking."

Wishbone moved to the edge of the canoe and stared at the bird. "It looks like Super Sleuth is in for mystery and adventure on Lost Lake. A loon in the flesh—I mean, in the feather."

A moment later, the loon dove below the surface, leaving behind only a small ring-shaped ripple.

"Let's do lunch sometime," Wishbone called out.

Luke steered the canoe in the direction of a rocky passageway. It separated two points of land.

"Heads up when we get to those narrows, Joe," Luke said. "There are boulders just below the surface."

"Is that Moose Cove beyond the rocks?" Joe asked.

"It sure is," Luke said.

Wishbone looked over the side of the canoe as they navigated through the narrows. Huge rocks lay just beneath the surface. Luke steered the canoe past them. Then they entered a large, oval-shaped cove. Luke pointed to the far shore.

"There are five camps in the cove," he said, reaching into his pocket. "Here's a map. But from here you can't see much more than the docks."

Joe unfolded the map and listened as Luke explained. "The camp on the far left wasn't there when your dad and I were kids. It gets rented out. A woman named Mrs. Joplin and her daughter have it for two weeks. I don't know anything about them. The camp next to theirs is the Talbots'."

Joe leaned forward. "My dad wrote in his journal that the main cabin's chimney was

visible through the trees. Yes—there it is!"
Wishbone heard him say.

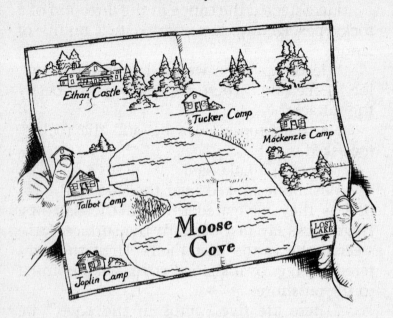

"Next is the camp that used to be owned
by the Tucker family," Luke said. "I'm sure
you read in Steve's journal about what happened to them. It sits empty now. On the far
right is the MacKenzie camp."

"Where's the fifth camp?" David asked.

"Straight back from the Talbot camp and
up the hill," Luke replied.

Wishbone looked up. He saw a large,
elegant white house built on a rock ledge.

"Not exactly what I'd call rustic," he said.

"It looks like a mansion," Joe said.

"That's one word for it," Luke answered. "Annette and Ethan Castle built it a few years ago. You'll see that folks on Lost Lake belong to one of two groups. There are the big-house-and-motorboat fans. And there are the cabin-in-the-woods people who like to paddle their own canoes."

A few minutes later, they tied the canoe to the Talbot dock. Wishbone was glad to have his four paws back on solid ground. He trotted ahead of Joe and David, who carried their bags. They followed Luke up a narrow path to the main cabin. Wishbone sniffed at the wood porch that ran along the front of the building. Inside, one large room served as living room, dining room, and kitchen. To the left was a fireplace, some comfortable chairs, and an electronic keyboard near the wall. To the right was a long table and benches. Against the back wall were a sink, stove, refrigerator, cabinets, and a doorway.

Luke led them through the doorway and into a tiny hallway. To the left was the bathroom. To the right, Wishbone saw a bedroom. He trotted inside the bedroom before anyone else, sniffing the air. "Super Sleuth arrives at the scene of the ancient crime."

Looking back over his shoulder, he saw Joe and David glance at each other as they entered the room.

"This was my grandparents' bedroom,"

Luke said with a little smile. "I use it now." He pointed to a small desk in the corner. "That's the desk where the Talbot watch was kept."

The small room also contained a bed, dresser, and lamp. A large acoustic guitar was lying on the window seat below the only window.

"I know you're eager to search the room for clues," Luke said. "But I want to show you the rest of the camp before we make dinner. Am I the only one who's hungry?"

"I've been too busy taking all this in to think about food," Joe said.

Wishbone scratched his back. "I can do both at once. I'm happy to give lessons . . . for a small but edible reward."

Luke opened the back door. Wishbone jumped outside ahead of his buddies. Luke showed them the wood shed attached to the side of the cabin and the tall, metal trash can in back. Luke kept his car parked in the clearing behind the cabin.

"Be sure to push the trash-can lid down really hard," Luke said. "Otherwise the raccoons will get inside."

They headed toward the dock once again, then turned left onto another path. It ran along the shore for a hundred feet and stopped in front of a tiny cabin.

"This is your home away from home," Luke said as he pushed open the door. "You can bring your bags down after dinner."

Wishbone leaped inside, smelling the old cedar boards. The cabin was just large enough for two single beds, a dresser, a small table, and a chair. There was a large window in each wall. From inside the cabin, only trees were visible, and on one side, the sparkling water beckoned.

"I really like this," Joe said.

Luke grinned. "So did your dad and I. When we turned eight, your great-grandfather built this cabin for us." He laughed, pointing to the wall above one bed. "I guess you could say we put our mark on the place."

"'S.T.'!" Joe said. He touched the initials carved into the wood above one bed. "And there's 'L.T.'" He pointed to the letters carved above the other bed.

Wishbone saw the look in Joe's eyes and knew what he was thinking. Joe was imagining his father standing in the same spot and listening to the breeze rustle leaves in the same trees.

Luke put a hand on Joe's shoulder. "I have one more thing to show you. I think Wishbone will find it interesting, too."

"In that case, *I'll* lead the way." Wishbone bounded outside. "Just tell me *which* way."

They returned to the dock and walked about two hundred feet past it.

"This is where the Talbot property ends," Luke said.

He pushed back some shrubs and pointed to a spit of land. It jutted into the water about thirty feet from them. At the end of it lay a loose mound of twigs, leaves, and grasses. A loon sat on the mound.

Luke spoke in a whisper. "It's the first time in years we've had a loon nest so close to us. The Loon Protection Society is monitoring all five nests. There were two eggs in each one, but half the eggs have already been destroyed."

"How?" David asked in a whisper.

Luke motioned them away from the shore.

"The male and female take turns sitting on the eggs," he explained. "If anything frightens the adult away from the nest, even for a few minutes, the eggs are at risk. Gulls, crows, and ravens will snatch them. So will skunks. But loon enemy number one is the raccoon."

Wishbone's fur bristled. "The masked bandit!"

They started back to the main cabin. The breeze had turned chilly.

"Don't get any nearer to the nest than we were," Luke said. "And try to keep Wishbone from scaring the loons. It's close to hatching time."

Wishbone shook his head. "Me? Scare them? I want to guard them! Guarantee their safety! I want to be their knight . . . in shining fur!"

He stopped walking and stood perfectly still in the middle of the path.

"I, Wishbone," he said, "do hereby take a solemn oath. I will protect and defend the loons of Lost Lake, their eggs, and their nests. I will defeat the masked bandits!"

Chapter Six

That evening, Joe was drying the last of the dinner dishes when the phone rang. Luke answered it.

"Talbot camp . . . Oh, hi there, Bill." Luke listened for a minute. "Yes, that crossed my mind, too . . . I'll call you right away if I come up with something . . . Thanks. 'Bye."

Luke sat down near the fireplace. He looked troubled but didn't speak right away. Joe caught David's eye. He wanted to ask about the call—and about the Talbot family watch. But he wasn't sure the time was right.

"It's gotten colder," he said to David. "Let's build a fire."

Luke didn't speak until a fire was crackling on the hearth. "That was the sheriff on the phone," he finally said. "He hasn't discovered anything about who wrecked my canoe. But he has a theory. Actually I'd already had the same idea."

"What is it?" David asked. He and Joe sat on the rug in front of the fireplace. Wishbone curled up next to them, raised his head, and sniffed the smoke-scented air.

"On Friday afternoon at two o'clock, the local bank is auctioning off the property next to ours—the old Tucker place," Luke explained. "The people who've owned it for the last few years went bankrupt. Someone might have destroyed my canoe to knock me out of the bidding. I don't have a lot of money, and I have to replace my canoe."

"You're bidding on the Tucker property?" Joe asked.

"I've got to save it from Ethan and Annette Castle," Luke explained. "As far as I'm concerned, all of Lost Lake is at stake."

"Why do the Castles want it?" David asked. "They already have that fancy place."

"They want lakefront property so they can dock their motorboats right here," Luke said. "Now they have to dock them in Woodwich. They love waterskiing. If they get the Tucker place, they plan to build a huge boathouse on the water. It'll look like a three-car garage. They'll have to dredge away land along the shore to create channels for the boats. If that weren't bad enough, they've applied for a permit to run a waterskiing school."

"That would ruin the cove!" Joe said.

Luke nodded. "It might also open up the entire lake for new development."

"Aren't there environmental laws protecting the lake?" David asked.

"The laws aren't strong enough," Luke said. He took off his wire-rimmed glasses and wiped the lenses. "Besides, some people believe more tourism on Lost Lake would create jobs for the year-round residents. I'm afraid the lake would lose all its magic. And the loons will be the first to go. The noise and pollution of motorboats disturb them. They get mangled in the propellers. And the waves swamp their nests."

"Can you outbid the Castles?" Joe asked. He hated to think of Lost Lake being ruined and the possible extinction of the loons.

"I doubt it," Luke replied. "But I'll try—with every penny I've got."

"Who else is bidding?" Joe asked. "Do—"

David interrupted him. "Should I get my computer and set up another case file?"

"Definitely," Joe said.

Two minutes later, David's laptop was set up on the floor in front of him. He read the title on the computer screen.

CASE FILE: SABOTAGED CANOE AND
AUCTION.STATUS: UNSOLVED.

He looked at Luke and Joe. "Okay, shoot."

"The auction was announced a month ago,"

Luke said. "It's also been posted in the *Woodwich Weekly*. Dozens of people might show up to bid. But I think the three most serious will be the Castles, the MacKenzies, and me

"The MacKenzies?" Joe asked. "Why?"

"They want to save the lake, just the way I do," Luke replied. "And Mac has always wanted a larger camp. He'll never get another opportunity like this."

"Maybe you could bid together," David suggested.

Luke shook his head. "I don't feel I can ask Mac to do that."

After seeing the strain between Luke and Mac, Joe could understand that.

"Do the Castles and MacKenzies know that you leave your canoe at the little dock in Woodwich?" Joe asked.

"Sure," Luke said.

"Then I guess they're suspects," Joe concluded.

Luke sighed and shook his head. "I decided a long time ago never to blame anyone for a crime until there's solid proof." He glanced at his watch. "It's getting late. I'll help carry your bags to your cabin. I'd better give you a couple of flashlights, in case you need them."

They made their way to their cabin along a narrow path. Joe listened to the sound of their footsteps on the packed earth. A canopy of trees hid the star-filled sky.

"There's another reason I want the Tucker property so badly," Luke said. "The Tuckers were the first family to homestead on Lost Lake in the nineteenth century. Tina Tucker's grandfather founded the Loon Protection Society. Her parents kept it going for years."

Luke paused for a moment and then added, "I haven't seen Tina since the summer we were all fourteen. But she and Steve were my best childhood friends. I can't let the Tucker place become a waterskiing school."

After saying good-night, Joe and David unpacked what they needed for the night. Joe stretched out on his bed and stared at the ceiling. With one hand, he rubbed Wishbone's head. David sat on his own bed with his back propped against the wall. He opened his computer and scrolled through the canoe case file.

"Now I've really got to solve the watch mystery," Joe said. "It's even more important than before. It's the only way to save Lost Lake!"

David looked up. "What do you mean?"

Joe turned to face him. "The Talbot watch is worth a lot of money. If we find it or catch the thief, Luke will have more money for his bid."

"We've got just two and a half days before the auction," David pointed out. "How about if we focus on Luke's canoe? Whoever destroyed it may have done it because he or she really wants the Tucker property. If we catch the person, that might mean one fewer bidder."

"It makes sense. But as far as I'm concerned, we've got to solve both cases by Friday," Joe said.

"I'll link the two case files in the computer right now." David's fingers tapped on the keyboard. After a few minutes' work, he paused and said, "Couldn't one of the Tuckers have taken the Talbot watch? Why was your dad so sure they weren't suspects? They lived so close by."

Joe got the journal out of his duffel bag.

"Listen to this. It's what my dad wrote the day after the watch was stolen."

Joe began to read:

August 1. We said good-bye to the Tuckers this morning. I wonder if I'll ever see Tina again . . .

Steve and Luke walked slowly along the wooded path to the Tucker property. It was ten in the morning. Steve finally broke the silence.

"I can't believe this is really happening. How could the Tuckers sell their camp? Lost Lake won't be the same without them."

"Gram won't say anything except that

there's been a family emergency," Luke said. "No one wants to talk about it. Not even Tina."

"It wouldn't be so bad if they were moving someplace nearby. But they're going all the way to Vancouver, Canada." Steve said. "That's on the other side of the continent."

Luke kicked a dead branch lying on the path. "This has been one lousy weekend," he muttered. "Yesterday the Talbot watch vanished. Today our best friend moves away. What a drag."

When they reached the Tucker camp, Gram and Pops were helping Tina's family load the last boxes into their station wagon. Tina nodded at Steve and Luke and then turned away. Mac had to work that morning, so he had stopped by earlier to say good-bye. Mrs. Tucker paused to give Gram a hug.

"Thanks again for helping us pack all day yesterday and this morning," she said. "I don't think we could have finished without you."

With a hard push, Mr. Tucker managed to close the wagon's rear door. "We'd better get this show on the road," he said.

A round of hugs and handshakes followed. Tina said good-bye to Steve and Luke last.

"You'll come back to visit next summer, won't you?" Steve asked.

Luke tried to smile. "You can't expect us to race across the cove without you."

"And you're the only one who can sing harmony with Luke on the guitar," Steve said.

Tina's black-brown eyes filled with tears. She hugged Steve and Luke quickly. Without saying a word, she got into the car. Everyone waved as the Tuckers started down the dirt road. But Tina didn't turn around to wave back.

Steve's voice was low. "Why do I keep thinking we'll never see her again?"

"How about adding this to the file?" David suggested to Joe. His fingers tapped the keys. "When the watch was taken, the Tuckers were at their camp. Gram was there, helping them."

"Good," Joe said.

David closed his computer. The night air was cold. The boys got under the wool blankets on their beds. Joe switched off the light. Wishbone curled up next to him.

Joe heard David's yawn. It was followed by a murmured, "'Night."

"'Night," Joe said, but his eyes stared into the darkness. He pictured his dad and Luke watching the Tuckers' car drive away . . . forever.

I wanted to solve a mystery that my dad couldn't figure out, Joe thought. *Now I want to save the whole lake. I wonder if my dad ever tried doing anything like this. I wonder if . . .*

Joe dozed off before he could finish his thought.

Wishbone listened to Joe's breathing until it became deep and regular.

"Sound asleep. Now for my nighttime security check."

The terrier hopped off the bed. Joe and David had left the door open a crack so he could get out. He nudged it with his nose and stepped outside. He heard the water lapping softly against the shore. The crickets hummed. A frog croaked.

"Ah, the sounds of the wild."

Wishbone trotted to the dock and looked out over the lake. The darkness of the water merged completely with the sky. Thousands of stars dotted the inky blackness. Each was a tiny point of glowing white light. Wishbone wagged his tail as he stared at the sky. But after a minute he turned away. "Super Sleuth's work is just beginning. There's an entire camp to patrol!"

Wishbone found the path to the main cabin. Halfway there, his ears pricked up. "What's that? Aha! Something in the woods. Near the main cabin."

He moved forward, listening carefully. He reached the clearing around the front porch, then stopped.

"There's the noise again! In back of the cabin now."

The terrier lowered his muzzle almost to the ground. He crept around to the left side of the cabin, sniffing . . . sniffing . . .

"Hmm. This is a familiar smell. A wild creature has been here! And Super Sleuth is on its trail."

Rustle! Snap! Thwack!

Wishbone's head jerked up. He leaped forward, racing in the direction of the sounds. He bounded around the corner of the cabin. An instant later, he came to a skidding stop. What he saw made his fur stand on end.

Wrestling with the garbage can was Loon Enemy Number One! A masked bandit! A raccoon!

Chapter Seven

"Hey, you! Get out of there!"

Wishbone barked as loudly as he could. The raccoon stood his ground. Wishbone crouched, aimed, and lunged at the raccoon. The animal sprang out of the way and bolted into the woods.

"You'd better not show your masked face around here again!" Wishbone called after him. "You're on my most-wanted list!"

He heard the raccoon scrambling away. The sound of twigs snapping and leaves rustling grew fainter. When it seemed safe, Wishbone trotted around to the other side of the cabin. Everything smelled and sounded secure. But when he reached the front porch, his ears picked up new sounds.

"That's coming from near the lake," he murmured, "where the sleeping cabin is! I'd better check on Joe and David."

Wishbone started down the path at a fast clip, hopping over branches and roots. As the noises ahead grew louder, the terrier was able to identify them.

"Footsteps," he said. "*People's* footsteps. And those voices are . . . Joe? David? Is that you?"

Wishbone blinked as a flashlight beam shone in his eyes.

"Wishbone, what's wrong?" Joe asked as he and David ran up to the terrier. "We heard you barking."

Joe knelt down and scratched Wishbone behind his ears. "You seem fine now. What was it, boy? Did a strange animal scare you?"

"Scare *me*? Uh, Joe, you've got that backwards," Wishbone said. "If you weren't giving me a good scratch, I'd consider myself insulted."

The three of them started back to their cabin. They hadn't taken more than few steps when Wishbone heard more rustling in the woods.

"What is this? Rush hour?" Wishbone stopped to listen.

Nothing.

He turned back to the path and took a few more steps. Again he heard rustling.

Wishbone spun around and faced the noise. He didn't hear anything else, but he saw a faint outline of something . . . or someone.

"Joe! David! Someone's there!"

Wishbone's yelping was sharp and loud. He kept at it, his eyes focused on the figure in the woods.

Just as Joe swung the beam of his flashlight toward Wishbone, the intruder took off. This time the rustling brush and snapping branches were loud enough for Joe and David to hear.

Joe swung the flashlight beam in the direction of the sounds. A human figure, dressed in yellow, was plunging through woods, away from them. A moment later, the figure vanished.

"Did you see that?" Joe asked.

David nodded. "It was someone wearing a yellow hooded jacket. Why would anyone be in these woods this late?"

Wishbone stretched out his neck and growled into the woods. "Good question. And Super Sleuth vows to find the answer!"

Joe woke up Wednesday morning to the sound of leaves rustling in the light wind. The early-morning sunlight flickered across his bed and the cabin floor.

As Joe threw off his blankets, Wishbone stretched his front legs. He jumped to the floor, his tail wagging.

"Come on, boy," Joe said. "I want to search the woods where we saw that prowler in the yellow jacket."

He glanced over at David's bed. David was still sleeping. Joe pulled on a pair of jeans and a T-shirt. Then he slipped out the door with Wishbone. They walked back along the path toward the main cabin. About halfway there, Joe stopped.

"This is pretty much where we were last night," he said.

Wishbone barked and bounded into the woods.

Joe followed and searched the area where he'd

seen the person in the yellow jacket. He looked around for footprints or anything that might have been dropped. After ten minutes, he gave up.

"Nothing," he muttered.

He and Wishbone returned to their cabin. When Joe pushed the door open, David was sitting up in bed.

"I've checked out the woods already," Joe told him.

"Find anything?" David asked.

"Nope. But maybe we should stake out the woods around the main cabin tonight," Joe said. "The person we saw might come around again." He took his bathing suit out of a dresser drawer. "Ready for a swim?"

David half-yawned and half-groaned. "What temperature did Luke say the water is?"

Joe grinned and tossed a towel at David. "Come on," he called as he jogged out the door with Wishbone. "We've got a lot to do."

David reached the dock just as Joe was getting ready to dive. The two boys stood poised side by side. The rippling water scattered sunlight over the lake like flashing diamonds. One deep breath . . . and they dove.

Splash! Joe's body plunged beneath the surface. Several seconds later, his head and shoulders emerged with a spray of drops. "Ee-oow-eee!"

"Aaahhh-ha!" David cried as he, too, surfaced.

Their shrieks echoed across the cove.

"Come on in, Wishbone!" Joe called out. "It's great!"

The dog stood at the water's edge, as if he were trying to make up his mind. Then he plunged into the water, splashing and yelping. Joe laughed when Wishbone scrambled out again a minute later.

Joe and David started swimming across the cove. The clear water felt like silk against Joe's skin. Winded, he stopped in the middle of the cove. David did the same. They treaded water and watched a small white cloud drift over the mountains.

"Do you realize how many times my dad must have done exactly this?" Joe said. "A thousand times. Even more."

"With Luke," David said. "Just like us. Well, not exactly. They could make it all the way across the cove and back."

Joe grinned. "We'll get there by the end of the week. At least that's my plan."

An hour later, the boys had finished breakfast. They returned to their cabin to get ready for a trip into Woodwich. Luke wanted to return the sheriff's canoe and buy a used one. Joe and David wanted to talk to the sheriff about the Talbot family watch. They also wanted to look around the little dock where Luke's canoe had been vandalized.

"Let's make a list of questions to ask the sheriff," Joe suggested. "You could print out a hard copy for us."

He and David went over possible questions and other information. David entered everything into the computer. He printed it out on a small, portable printer.

"Time to get going," Luke called from the dock.

David folded the paper and put it in the pocket of his windbreaker.

A half-hour later, they arrived at Woodwich. This time Luke used the town dock. He tied the borrowed canoe to one of the posts and then checked his watch.

"Let's meet back here in an hour and a half," he said.

"Sounds good," Joe agreed. He, David, and Wishbone walked straight to the sheriff's office. Sheriff Eastwood was talking on the phone when they arrived. He gave them a friendly wave and motioned them to sit down.

As soon as the sheriff hung up, he said, "Nice to see you boys again. Anything I can help you with?"

"Well, I found a journal my father kept the summer he was my age," Joe began. "That's how I learned about Lost Lake and all the time he spent here. You said you knew him and the rest of the family. So I wondered if you could tell me more about that summer. It seems like a lot happened."

The sheriff nodded in a sympathetic way, smoothing his gray moustache with his fingers.

"Which summer was it exactly?" he asked.

"The summer the Tucker family moved away," Joe replied. "Mac MacKenzie bought a VW bus and drove cross-country. And my family's heirloom watch was stolen."

The sheriff leaned back in his chair. He folded his arms across his chest. "Hmm, the summer the Tuckers left. Yep, I remember it well. It was sad to see them go after their long history here. A real pity."

"Why did they leave?" Joe asked. "My dad didn't know."

"Mr. Tucker had debts he couldn't pay," the sheriff said. "They moved to Vancouver because Mrs. Tucker's family lived there. It was a good place for them to make a fresh start."

"Did anyone know about the debts that summer?" Joe asked.

"No, but the news got out over time," the sheriff said. "I suppose some of us guessed it that summer. But no one wanted to talk about it—especially not the Tuckers. Losing the family home was a terrible blow for them."

Joe nodded. "My dad was afraid he'd never see Tina Tucker again. I guess he never did."

A smile flickered across Sheriff Eastwood's

face. "They were great friends, your dad, Luke, and Tina. Mac, too. It would have been nice to see them all here together as adults."

No one spoke for a moment.

"I remember the morning the Tuckers left," the sheriff continued. "I stopped by very early to say good-bye. Tina was digging a hole near the back wall of their cabin."

"Digging?" Joe leaned forward. "Do you know why?"

"I didn't want to ask what she was doing," the sheriff continued. "She looked so sad. But I assumed she was probably planting something. A kind of reminder to others of who once lived there."

Or maybe, just maybe, Joe thought, *it was something else altogether.*

"As for Mac," the sheriff went on. "Well, he made it back from California safe and sound. Much to his mother's relief. He drove that VW bus until it was a heap of scrap metal. Mac loved that crazy thing. The same way Pat loves his motorcycle. Like father, like son."

"What about the Talbot family watch?" Joe asked.

Sheriff Eastwood shook his head. "Vanished. Seemed to disappear into thin air. No trace of it since then."

"Do you think an outsider could have taken it?" David asked. "Someone who was passing by?"

"It's very unlikely," the sheriff answered. "The Talbot camp is isolated. Strangers don't go walking in those private woods."

The sheriff glanced at the clock. "I've got more phone calls to make right now. But feel free to stop by again. I hadn't thought about that summer for a long time. A blast from the past for me."

Joe and David thanked the sheriff. As Joe was walking out the door, he turned and asked, "Do you remember exactly where Tina was digging the morning she left?"

Sheriff Eastwood looked up from his papers and thought for a moment. "To the right of the cabin's back door, as I recall. I'd say three or four feet."

From the sheriff's office, Joe, Wishbone, and David headed for the little dock where Luke's canoe had been wrecked.

"Are you thinking what I'm thinking?" David asked Joe.

"You mean that the Tuckers had a motive for taking the watch," Joe answered. "They really needed money. But if they *did* take the watch, it didn't help them stay at Lost Lake."

"I know," David said. A moment later he added, "Shouldn't we check out the place where Tina was digging.

"Definitely." Joe shook his head, thinking the whole thing over. "It's strange," he said. "I mean, why would Tina take the watch and then bury it? She was about to move thousands of miles away. But it also seems weird for her to be digging that morning."

David shrugged. "Maybe we'll find out more when we check out the Tuckers' camp."

No one else was around when they reached the little dock. No boats were tied to the posts. Joe and David began examining the dock carefully. Wishbone sniffed around the grass and shrubs on shore.

"What are we looking for?" David asked.

"Anything unusual." Joe walked slowly up and down the dock, scouring every inch. "Anything that's been disturbed or doesn't seem to belong—"

Joe suddenly stopped talking and looked at Wishbone. "What are you digging up, boy?"

Wishbone was pawing at the leaves and grass that edged the dock. He let out a sharp bark, pushing into the spot with his muzzle.

"I think he's found something!" David said.

Joe reached Wishbone in two quick steps. As he bent down, Wishbone lifted his head. Sunlight glinted off the shiny metal item clamped between Wishbone's teeth.

"It's a key ring." Joe took the metal ring out of Wishbone's mouth. One key hung from it, along with a shiny metal tag. Joe whistled under his breath. "Check out the tag," he told

David. "It has a picture of a castle on it."

David's eyes opened wide. "Do you think it belongs to . . . "

Joe nodded. "Ethan and Annette Castle."

Chapter Eight

Wishbone sniffed at the key ring in Joe's hand. "Yes! Super Sleuth makes an important breakthrough in the case!"

"Great find, Wishbone," David said.

"It's all in a day's work." Wishbone wagged his tail as David rubbed his head. "Edible rewards, however, will be accepted."

Joe put the key ring in his jeans pocket. "We'd better pay a visit to the Castles this afternoon." He checked his watch. "We should get going. It's time to meet Luke at the town dock."

When Joe, David, and Wishbone got there, Luke was waiting. He pointed out an old-style aluminum canoe that was bobbing in the water.

"She's patched here and there," he said. "One seat's a little loose. But she's watertight and sturdy. And she's ours. Climb in."

As soon as they got back to the Talbot camp, Joe and David wolfed down sandwiches and borrowed a shovel from Luke. Wishbone trotted at their heels as they headed for the camp that had belonged to the Tuckers.

"We've got so little time," Joe said as they followed the path through the woods. "It's noon, and the auction is at two on Friday. That's just over forty-eight hours."

"Let's hit the pavement—well, actually, the path." Wishbone kicked up his paws and raced on ahead.

Soon he came to a clearing around a large cabin. Wishbone's ever-sensitive nose told him no one had been living at the camp for a while. There were no lingering food smells, no whiff of garbage. In addition, he could see that the paint on the window frames was peeling. He peered through the large glass pane of the front door. The main room was completely empty and dusty.

"I can't believe it!" Joe's call came from the back of the cabin. "Someone beat us here!"

"Hey, wait for Super Sleuth!" Wishbone ran around to where Joe and David stood, a few feet to the right of the back door. The ground near them looked uneven. Loose dirt was scattered around.

"Someone's been digging!" Wishbone ran over to the patch of earth and began sniffing. "An ancient and noble canine activity. But in this case, Super Sleuth is picking up a *human* scent."

David and Joe knelt down next to Wishbone.

"This is spooky," David said.

"You can say that again," Joe muttered. "Who else could know about Tina Tucker digging here? That was years ago." He glanced around uneasily. "Do you think the person who was digging is still around?"

Wishbone stretched his neck out. His whiskers quivered.

"Hmm, yes. There's something in the air. Or is it . . . some*one*?"

David touched the loose dirt. "This could have been dug up a while ago. If there wasn't a heavy rain, the ground would stay just like this."

Wishbone sniffed the dirt again. "Nope. Take it from a pro. This hole is freshly dug."

This reminds me of Tom Sawyer, Detective, he thought. *Tom was trying to find a dead body that had disappeared. Whom did he turn to? A dog. A neighbor's bloodhound. The dog did some sniffing and digging—and got the job done.*

Wishbone positioned himself right over the loose earth. He leaned forward and stretched out his front legs.

"There might not be anything buried here. But Super Sleuth knows it never hurts to dig deeper."

His hind legs began churning. Dirt flew out from under them.

"Watch out!" Joe said. He covered his face with his arm. He and David scrambled out of the way.

Several minutes later, Wishbone had dug down to hard-packed earth. He had produced a good-sized hole. Joe and David inspected it carefully and sifted through the loose dirt.

"Nothing," Joe said. "Thanks for trying, Wishbone."

Panting, Wishbone lay down on a patch of grass. "Can't win 'em all."

"Let's look around the rest of the cabin," Joe suggested. "Maybe whoever was here left something."

David took off his windbreaker and tossed it to the ground. "I'll do that while you fill in the hole."

Wishbone rested on the grass. When David returned a few minutes later, he shook his head.

"I didn't see anything," David said. He took the sheet of questions and a pen out of his jacket pocket. "I'd better make some notes on all this."

Wishbone stood up, whiskers quivering. "There it is again. Someone else is here. I can feel it!"

He walked slowly toward the woods behind the cabin. He paused now and then to sniff. It was the same scent he'd smelled earlier. At the edge of the woods, he stopped and listened.

"Yes! In there! I hear someone!"

Wishbone leaped foward, barking. He'd taken just a few steps when a teenage girl appeared on a path. She carried a water bottle for hiking.

"Hi, there, pooch," she said. Then she stepped past Wishbone and moved toward the clearing where the Tuckers' cabin was. Wishbone followed her. At the edge of the woods, the girl stepped on a branch that was lying on the path.

Snap!

Looking ahead, Wishbone saw Joe and David spin around. Joe was still holding the shovel. David reached down on the ground and quickly stuffed his pen and paper into his jacket pocket. Wishbone could see that Joe was observing the girl carefully.

She was about fourteen, medium-tall, thin, and tanned. She kept her short, dark hair pushed behind her ears. She wore shorts, a long-sleeved shirt, and hiking boots.

"Sorry," the girl said. She had a very confident manner. "I didn't mean to barge in on you. I'd heard this camp was empty. So I thought it would be okay to hike through the woods nearby."

Wishbone trotted over to Joe. "Don't believe her, Joe! She's been watching us for a while."

Joe continued watching the girl. When he didn't respond, Wishbone sighed.

"Nobody listens to the dog."

"This place *is* empty," Joe said to the girl. "We're staying at the camp next to this one. The Talbot camp."

"And you're gardening here?" the girl asked with a teasing smile. "Or digging for buried treasure?"

Joe glanced down at the shovel. "Uh, well . . ." He took a step forward and held out his hand. "I'm Joe Talbot. This is David Barnes. And that's Wishbone, my dog."

"I'm Ally Joplin," the girl said. She shook hands with the boys and rubbed the top of Wishbone's head.

"Hmm. Nice touch," Wishbone said.

Ally continued. "I'm staying at the camp on the other side of yours."

"Oh, right," David said. "We heard some-one was renting that place."

"I've never been to Lost Lake before," Ally said. "It's pretty awesome. Do you come here every summer?"

Joe shook his head. "This is our first time. But my dad spent summers here when he was a kid. His cousin owns the Talbot place now. The camp's been in the family for ages."

"Lucky you," Ally said.

She picked up a short, thick stick. "Here, Wishbone." She tossed the stick in a high arc. It landed all the way across the clearing.

"You like to play? I happen to be an expert at stick toss," Wishbone said and bounded off.

He returned with the stick in time to hear Ally ask, "Have you seen the loon nest?"

"We went to see it yesterday when we got here," David answered. "The chicks could hatch any day now."

Ally looked past them toward the lake. Slivers of sparkling water were visible between the trees. "I'd love to see a loon chick."

After a moment, she turned to the boys. "Well, back to the woods for me. Nice meeting you."

"You, too," Joe said.

"See you around," David added.

Just as Ally reached the woods path, she called out, "Happy gardening—or whatever you're doing."

As soon as she was out of earshot, David asked, "Do you think she heard us talking before we noticed her?"

"I doubt it," Joe answered. He picked up the shovel. "I can't think of anything else we need to do here. So let's go up to the Castles' place. I want to see what they know about the key ring."

Wishbone jumped to his feet. "Excellent idea! Super Sleuth will lead the way."

When they got to the Talbot camp, Wishbone heard music coming from inside the main cabin.

"Mom told me Luke's a musician," Joe said. He headed to the shed to return the shovel. "Let's not disturb him."

"No problem! I always respect artists at work." Wishbone trotted behind the cabin. His nose led him to the path that rose up the hill behind the Talbot property. "This must be the way to the Castles'. Follow me!"

They had walked a few minutes when Wishbone heard David hit his palm against his forehead.

"My windbreaker! I left it at the Tucker camp. I'd better get it before I forget about it completely." He started jogging down the hill.

"I won't be long," he called over his shoulder.

Joe sat down. He leaned his back against a thick pine tree. Wishbone lay down next to him and nudged Joe's hand. "This is the perfect opportunity for a head rub . . . ahhh . . . just right!"

Somewhere a woodpecker was tapping on a tree trunk. The hollow-sounding taps made a faint echo. The minutes slipped by.

"Joe!"

Wishbone raised his head to see David hurrying up the path, carrying his windbreaker.

"You're not going to believe what happened," he said. He stopped a moment to catch his breath. "I found my jacket right where I left it—near the cabin. But guess what? The page of questions and notes is gone! Someone took it from my pocket!"

"Maybe it fell out," Joe said.

David shook his head. "I looked all over for it. Besides, the pockets in this jacket are really deep."

"Who could even see the jacket near the cabin?" Joe asked. "It's in the middle of the woods."

"Maybe someone who's interested in buying the cabin came to check the place out and found my jacket," David pointed out. "The person could have looked in the pockets to find out whose jacket it was."

Joe stood up and brushed off his jeans. "Whoever has the paper knows just about everything we know about the watch, the canoe, and the auction," he said.

The fur along Wishbone's spine bristled. "Sounds like trouble for Super Sleuth."

No one spoke as they continued up the hill. Soon Wishbone trotted out of the woods and onto a wide ridge. The Castles' large, white house loomed up in front of them. It stood in the middle of a lawn framed by flower beds and well-trimmed shrubs.

"Not your typical Moose Cove camp," David said.

Joe pointed to an unfinished wooden platform that wrapped around one side of the house. "Looks like they're building a new deck."

They walked along a gravel path that led to the back door. A van and a shiny jeep stood in the driveway.

Joe knocked on the frame of the screen door. Wishbone heard footsteps. A moment later, a woman opened the door.

"Mrs. Castle?" Joe asked.

"Yes."

The woman was tall, elegant, and in her mid-thirties. She wore her blond hair pulled back in a French twist. She had on a strawberry-colored sleeveless sweater and tailored black pants.

Joe introduced himself. "I'm Joe Talbot. My friend David and I are staying with Luke Talbot down the hill."

"Oh, hello," the woman said. "I'm Annette Castle. Luke told us he was expecting guests." She hesitated a moment. "Well, would you like to come in?"

She motioned for the boys to step inside. They entered a small mudroom filled with jackets, rain slickers, boots, and beach things. As Wishbone followed, he looked up at Annette.

"Hi! My name's Wishbone. And if you're handing out snacks—"

"I really don't like animals in the house," Annette said, frowning at him. "Can your dog wait here?"

Joe nodded and turned to Wishbone. "Sorry, boy. You'll have to stay here."

"Super Sleuth banned from an investigation scene? It's unheard of!" Wishbone protested.

The door leading inside closed right in front of Wishbone's nose.

Joe and David followed Annette Castle from the mudroom into a large kitchen. From there, Joe could see the vast living room. A wall of windows and glass doors gave a sweeping view of the mountains and lake. Tiny, tree-covered islands dotted the water's silver-blue surface.

"You have a great view," David said.

"Yes, it's quite grand," Annette replied. "That's why we're enlarging our deck. We do a lot of entertaining. Pat MacKenzie is building it for us. Have you met the MacKenzies?"

"Yesterday," Joe said. "Right after we got here."

The back door swung open. Through the kitchen door, Joe saw a tall, heavyset man walk in. He had straight blond hair, and he wore shorts, a tennis shirt, and tennis shoes. The man put away his racquet and balls and strode into the kitchen.

"This is my husband, Ethan Castle," Annette said.

The boys introduced themselves and shook hands with Mr. Castle.

"What can we do for you?" Annette asked, glancing at the clock.

Joe held out the key ring. "We found this near the little dock in Woodwich. We thought it might belong to you."

Ethan took the key from Joe and inspected it. "As a matter of fact, it does. It's our spare house key." He hung it on a hook near the door where other keys were hanging. "I don't know how it got down to the little dock. I wasn't there. Were you?" he asked his wife.

She shook her head. "I never use that dock."

Joe watched them closely. "That's where we found Luke's new canoe," he said. "Someone had smashed up the entire bottom."

"We heard about that," Annette said. She leaned against the polished granite countertop. "I don't understand how such vandalism could have happened. Or how our key ring could have gotten down to the dock."

"I hate to cut this visit short," Ethan said. "But Annette and I have a load of wood to pick up at the lumber yard. Pat MacKenzie was supposed to get it. But he called earlier to say something's come up. He's busy this afternoon."

They all walked out of the kitchen together. As they passed through the mudroom, Annette Castle took a jacket off one of the pegs. A flash of color caught Joe's eye. He quickly nudged David with his elbow and nodded to where the jackets and coats were hanging. David looked in that direction. He breathed in sharply.

Underneath the jacket Annette had taken hung another jacket—a yellow hooded jacket.

Chapter Nine

Wishbone jumped up and sniffed at the yellow jacket. "It's just like the one we saw last night on that person in the woods. Good eye, Joe!"

The boys said good-bye to the Castles. Wishbone noticed that his friends moved faster than usual as they headed for the path that led down the hill.

"We'd better keep an eye on them," Joe said under his breath. "If that was Mr. or Mrs. Castle in the woods last night, they might be planning something else."

"Like more sabotage to knock Luke out of the bidding," David said. "They sure wanted us out of there."

Wishbone sniffed the air. "And they wouldn't even let me in! Is that any way to treat the dog? Super Sleuth is going to keep a close watch on those two . . ."

"The case files are all updated," David said later that afternoon.

Joe went over to the table in the main cabin where David had set up his computer. "Great," he said. "I can't wait to tell Luke everything we found out."

The cabin had been empty when Joe, David, and Wishbone returned from the Castles'. They had found a note from Luke. He had gone to town to do errands. But as David closed his laptop, Luke stepped in through the front door. He put a package wrapped in paper on the table.

"Fresh fish to grill for dinner," he said. "And I'm famished. Let's get the chow on the table pronto. You can fill me in on your investigations while we eat."

During dinner, Joe and David described the afternoon's events. Luke listened carefully. "I don't suppose a key chain is proof that they destroyed my canoe," he said. "But it sure is suspicious. Especially if one of the Castles was in the woods down here last night." Luke shook his head. "I wish I'd known about this when I saw Annette and Ethan this afternoon. I stopped at the lumber yard for nails, and they were there. They were picking up a load of lumber."

"If they did wreck your canoe, we need to prove it by Friday," Joe said.

David nodded. "There's so much we need to find out—about the Castles *and* about the Talbot watch."

After dinner, Luke showed Joe and David several shelves of old scrapbooks. "These are our camp logs," he said. "Gram Talbot liked to record all the events on the lake. I've kept up the tradition. So there's a log for every summer. There are lots of photos and everything else that could be glued down. We wrote about hikes, swimming races—you name it. And we always asked our guests to sign the current log."

Joe stared at the albums lined up on the shelves. He found the log from the summer when the watch had disappeared. "I'd like to go through all of them," he said. "But I'd better start with this one. We've got so little time before the auction."

"I'll look at the log from the summer after that," David said. "There might be some follow-up about the watch."

Joe settled into an armchair near the fireplace. Wishbone climbed onto his lap. David sat at the table, while Luke played on the keyboard. He turned the volume low.

Once again, real time seemed to fade away for Joe as he paged through the log. He studied each photo: Tina and his dad playing volleyball in the water. Gram and Luke playing chess on the porch, the whole family hiking up a mountain to pick blueberries. Joe smiled when he found the photo of his dad, Mac, and Pops holding up the large bass. As he looked at the pictures, he could almost smell the pine-scented air. He could almost hear the splash of someone diving into the water and feel the cold spray on his shoulders. He could almost hear his dad's high-spirited laugh.

Joe found a page dated August first. He started to read an entry in Gram's handwriting.

It's a very sad day for us and for Lost Lake. The Tucker family has moved away. We'll all miss them.

Joe wanted to show the page to David. Before he could, Wishbone suddenly stood up and started barking.

"What's happening?" Luke asked, looking up from his keyboard.

"He must hear something in the woods," Joe said.

Wishbone jumped off the chair and ran to the door, still barking.

Joe heard footsteps on the porch stairs. Luke got up and turned on the porch light. Through the screen door, Joe saw Mac and Pat MacKenzie approaching.

"This is a surprise," Luke said, opening the door wide. "Come on in."

The MacKenzies stepped inside. They both looked serious, even grim.

"Have a seat," Luke said. He pointed to the chairs and sat down himself.

Mac shook his head. "No, thanks. We can't stay long." He glanced around the room as if he hadn't seen it for a while. He ran one hand through his unruly hair. Pat looked down at his heavy leather boots.

"We heard about your canoe when we were in town today," Mac said. "Something else has happened, too. Someone stole Pat's motorcycle."

Luke's mouth fell open. "What in the world is going on at Lost Lake?"

"Pat mentioned that he saw you in Woodwich late this afternoon," Mac continued. "I wondered if you noticed anything unusual when you were there."

Luke thought for a minute. "No, everything seemed pretty normal. Did you report the theft to Bill Eastwood?"

"Right away," Mac said.

"When did it happen?" Luke asked, turning to Pat. "Where was the bike stolen?"

Pat leaned against the door frame. "I guess it happened sometime between three and seven," he said. "I left the bike at a friend's house, Gerry Rich. He lives on the edge of town. When a bunch of us go out together, I leave my bike there, behind the tool shed. Then we take Gerry's car."

"Does anyone know you leave your bike there?" Luke asked.

"All my friends, I guess," Pat said. "I never thought it had to be a major secret. I probably told some of the people I work for. The Millers and the Castles, maybe."

Joe caught the quick glance David shot at him at the mention of the Castles' name.

"There's another reason I wanted to talk about this," Mac said. He rubbed his chin and looked at Luke. "I wonder if the canoe and the motorcycle might have something to do with the auction on Friday. Everyone knows we're both bidding."

Luke nodded. "The boys and I have talked about that. Bill Eastwood mentioned it to me, too."

"The Castles are bidding at the auction," Joe said. He opened his mouth to say more, then stopped and glanced at Luke.

"Go on, Joe. You might as well tell the MacKenzies what you and David found," Luke said. "But let's be careful about this. It could all turn out to be pure coincidence."

Mac and Pat listened carefully while Joe told them about the Castles' key ring and the yellow hooded jacket.

"And I saw Annette and Ethan in town this afternoon," Luke added. "So I suppose they could have stolen your motorcycle, Pat."

"Everyone knows how much they want the Tucker property," Mac said. "But I don't understand why they would sabotage us this way. They can just outbid us." He stuffed his hands into his jacket pockets. "Well, it's getting late."

Luke stood up. "Let's keep each other informed about anything else that happens. And thanks a lot for stopping by."

The MacKenzies said good-night and left. Luke stepped out onto the porch, watching as they walked away.

"It's a crystal-clear night," he said when he came back in. "Before you boys hit the sack, you should look at the sky from the dock. The stars are amazing."

Joe nodded. "We'll do that. We're going to be up for a while anyway. We want to check out the woods in case there's someone prowling around like last night."

"Be careful, boys," Luke said.

The boys went down to their cabin to get heavy sweaters. They walked as silently as possible. Now and then, they shone their flashlights into the woods. They didn't see or hear anyone. Joe noticed that Wishbone was also quiet. He trotted alongside with his tail wagging.

Joe switched off his flashlight when they

got to the end of the dock. The lake was still and smooth. Above, the star-studded sky seemed to go on forever.

"I've never seen the Milky Way so clearly," David said. "It looks like a huge streak of glowing white powder across the sky." He laughed. "That's not very scientific. But that's how it looks to me tonight."

Joe sat down on the edge of the dock. Wishbone stretched out next to him. For a long time, Joe just watched and listened. Finally he said, "I guess I understand why my dad loved this place so much."

Wishbone stretched out his front legs and arched his back. "Time to limber up for my night rounds. See you guys later!"

Leaving Joe and David, he trotted off the dock. Ahead of him were three paths.

"Left for the loon nest. Straight ahead for the main cabin. Right for the cabin," he said. "I'll go . . . left."

Wishbone sniffed as he walked along. "Mixed vegetation . . . harmless small mammal . . . trace of Luke . . . hint of—"

Wishbone froze. He sniffed long and deep. With a growl rumbling deep in his throat, he leaped forward. He started running down the path.

The smell of masked bandits! It's getting stronger! I've got to reach the loon nest in time!

Wishbone almost tripped on a vine but

kept himself from tumbling. He dashed on. As he got to the halfway point, he heard rustling up ahead. The rustling quickly turned into a louder, scrambling noise. Wishbone was bounding down the path. He was getting close.

Aa-o-aa-o-aa-o-aa!

The high-pitched loon alarm-call! The spit of land was just up ahead. Wishbone sprang forward.

Splash!

Wishbone knew that an adult loon had thrown itself into the water. And that meant . . .

"The nest . . . it's unprotected!"

All of a sudden the terrier heard human voices. "What's that? Watch it! Get out of here!"

A large animal streaked across the path right in front of Wishbone.

"Raccoon!" Wishbone barked loudly as he lunged.

Aagh! Oof! Ehgh! Something stopped him in midair. His legs churned without touching the ground.

"Let me go!" Wishbone shouted.

Chapter Ten

Twisting and turning, Wishbone struggled to get free. It was no use. Someone had grabbed him around the belly. Someone else had his collar in a tight grip.

"Hey, you've got the wrong guy!" Wishbone said. "You want the one in the fur mask. The one who just escaped into the woods."

"You mustn't disturb the loons," a woman's voice scolded.

Wishbone didn't recognize the voice. But he caught a familiar scent. He stopped struggling so he could get a good, deep whiff of the hands holding onto his collar. He knew those hands. He sniffed again.

It's that girl, the one who was hiking! Ally Joplin!

"What are we going to do about this dog?" It was the unfamiliar voice.

Ally rubbed Wishbone's head.

"Don't worry, Mom," she said. "This is Wishbone. He belongs to one of the boys I met this afternoon. He's really cute and smart—"

"True," Wishbone said.

"And good."

"Also true," Wishbone said.

"We just have to talk to the boys," Ally continued. "They'll keep Wishbone away from the nest."

"Wait a minute," Wishbone protested. "I'm the loons' official knight in shining fur!"

"I'd feel more comfortable if we delivered the dog to the boys in person. And talked to them right now," said Ally's mom.

"I'm not the troublemaker here!" Wishbone

said. "I wish you people spoke basic Dog. We'd save a lot of time."

He started off in the direction of the Talbot camp. Ally and her mother followed him to the dock. When they got there, Wishbone bounded along the wood planks to Joe and David. "Don't listen to them, Joe! I was trying to save the loons!"

The boys stood up when they saw two new figures walking toward them. Joe switched on his flashlight, directing the beam downward. "Ally?"

"Hi, guys," Ally said. "This is my mom, Mrs. Joplin. Mom, this is Joe and David."

Mrs. Joplin shook hands with the boys. In the dim light, Wishbone saw that she was tall and slim like her daughter. She wore her graying hair very short.

"Your terrier gave the loons quite a scare," Mrs. Joplin said. "The nesting bird dove into the water."

Wishbone looked up sharply at Ally's mom. "Am I the only one who saw that raccoon? That's who scared the loon, not me!"

"You probably shouldn't let Wishbone wander around alone at night," Mrs. Joplin went on. "At least until the eggs hatch. It won't be long—just a couple of days."

Joe nodded. "That's a good idea. We'll keep him with us."

"How am I going to make my nighttime rounds?" Wishbone asked. "Helllooo! Will someone please listen to the dog?"

Before dawn on Thursday, Wishbone's eyes fluttered open. He was lying next to Joe in their cabin.

"Super Sleuth is awake. But why at this hour?" he wondered.

As soon as he tried closing his eyes again, he knew why. Joe was awake and restless. Wishbone moved closer to him on the bed. Joe stroked his back.

"Just a day and a half before the auction," Joe said in a low voice. "I keep thinking about saving the lake. And about my dad. It's so easy to imagine him here in this cabin."

He reached over the edge of the bed. He found his flashlight and his dad's journal on the floor where he'd left them. He rolled over to face the wall in order not to disturb David. He switched on the flashlight and opened the journal.

August 2. I've been thinking a lot about Tina and the last time we talked. It was the night before she left. Well, technically, it was morning . . .

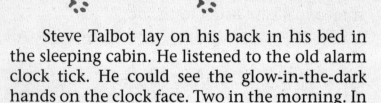

Steve Talbot lay on his back in his bed in the sleeping cabin. He listened to the old alarm clock tick. He could see the glow-in-the-dark hands on the clock face. Two in the morning. In the other bed, Luke turned over in his sleep.

I'm never going to fall asleep, Steve thought. *I can't get my mind off the missing watch. And in just a few hours, we'll be saying good-bye to the Tuckers.*

He lay there without moving, trying to relax. The clock's ticking seemed to grow louder. It made Steve's head throb. He threw off his blankets.

I might as well get up.

He pulled on his patched bell-bottomed jeans and a faded Beatles sweatshirt. He shoved his feet into a pair of tennis sneakers without laces. Grabbing a flashlight, he stepped silently out the door.

Steve didn't need to switch on the flashlight. The nearly full moon cast soft shadows on the ground. He took the path to the dock and walked out to the end of it. He stared into the darkness of the water. Every time the breeze picked up, the trees along the shore responded with a rush of rustling leaves.

Then Steve heard something else—a faint rippling sound. He looked up just in time to see a canoe slip out of the cove. It passed through the rocky narrows and disappeared as it entered the main lake.

That's weird, Steve thought. *Who'd be out on the lake in the middle of the night?*

His mind immediately jumped to the missing watch.

Is someone trying to hide the watch–or leave the lake with it? Does that make any sense? He shrugged. *Nothing seems too strange to me right now.*

Steve turned and hurried straight to the main cabin. He grabbed one of the canoe paddles stored on the porch. Back at the dock, he pushed a canoe into the water. He moved quickly and quietly. Stepping into the boat, he sat on the backseat and began paddling across the cove.

The wind was getting stronger. Several large clouds had gathered in the sky. As they blew past the moon, they blotted out the light. Steve watched the clouds thicken as he reached the middle of the cove. They filled the sky. Everything around him was plunged into darkness.

He switched on his flashlight and laid it on the canoe's front seat. It gave him enough light to steer toward the narrows. He paddled faster.

His canoe slid past the rocks and entered the main lake. The wind was gusting harder there. The water was choppy, swelling and dipping. The boat bobbed up and down. Steve hesitated.

Are we in for a storm? Or is this going to blow past the lake?

Just then, his flashlight beam revealed something in the distance.

The other canoe!

Steve quickly turned his own canoe toward it and began paddling again. The distance between the two boats began to close.

That's odd, Steve thought. *The other canoe isn't moving forward. It's just bobbing on the water.* He squinted, trying to see more. His heart skipped a beat.

There's no one in that boat!

Steve worked hard to stay on course. The wind pushed his canoe in one direction, then another. Thunder rumbled in the distance. The first heavy drops of rain splattered on the aluminum seats.

As he approached the other canoe, Steve steered sharply to the right. His canoe glided alongside the drifting one. He reached out and grabbed the side of the other canoe. As his hand touched the cold metal, he leaned forward and looked inside.

"Ahhh!" he gasped.

In the darkness, he saw a body. It lay stretched out on the bottom of the canoe. Steve froze.

Suddenly the body sat up. It screamed, making Steve jump. His heart pounded.

"Tina!" he cried.

Tina gasped. "Steve! You scared me to death!"

"I scared *you?*" Steve said. "You almost gave me a heart attack! What are you doing out here?"

Tina switched on her flashlight. Her face looked strained and pale to Steve. He didn't think it was just because of the fright he had given her.

"I couldn't sleep," she said. "I decided to say a last good-bye to the lake. I was lying out here, feeling the boat rock on the water. I was trying to think about some things. Then a face lunged at me. Yours! By the way, what are *you* doing out here?"

"I couldn't sleep either," Steve admitted. "I went down to the dock and happened to see a canoe leaving the cove. That seemed odd, so I decided to follow it. I didn't know it was you."

Tina laughed. "The youth sleuth is at it again. Chills and thrills on Lost Lake. Wait till we tell Luke about this." She paused. Her voice lost any trace of joy. "Well, you can tell him. In a few hours, I'll be past history on Lost Lake."

"Tina—"

A flash of lightning blazed in the sky. It lit up the lake for an instant. Almost immediately a loud crack of thunder seemed to shatter the atmosphere.

Steve jumped. "That was really close. Too close. We'd better get off the lake."

"You're not kidding," Tina said. "We're like lightning rods out on the water in these metal canoes."

Steve leaned forward and grabbed the rope attached to the front of Tina's canoe. "Let's both paddle in one boat," he said. "We'll go faster."

Tina helped him tie the rope to the back of his canoe. Steve held her paddle and flashlight while she climbed from her boat to his. She took the front seat, and they began paddling hard and fast. Tina's canoe trailed behind them.

The scattered raindrops quickly turned into a downpour. Wind blew the water in their faces. Tina's long hair swirled around her head. In just a few minutes, water was streaming down their soaked clothing.

The wind was strong enough to make white-capped waves. Swells of water rose high around the shallow canoe. Steve steered right into the waves. They slapped against the metal, jolting Tina and Steve. Yet Steve knew this was safer than letting the waves hit the side of the boat. A wave smashing against the side could swamp the canoe.

Steve gritted his teeth and plunged his paddle into the churning water.

"Stroke, back. Stroke, back," he said to himself. "Harder . . . *harder!*"

Another flash of lightning lit up the sky. A clap of thunder followed.

This is really bad news, Steve thought.

"We've got to hang in there," Tina shouted over her shoulder.

"As soon as we get into the cove, I'm heading for the nearest shore," Steve shouted back. "We can't risk trying to get to one of the docks."

"Right," Tina called.

Every minute or so, Steve switched on his flashlight. He wanted to check their course. They both knew that part of the lake like the backs of their hands. But Steve also knew that the wind and waves might throw them off. The small, bobbing beam of light didn't reveal much at first. All Steve saw was driving rain. But finally it showed the rocky narrows that led into Moose Cove.

"Hold onto your paddle," Steve shouted. "This is going to be a bumpy ride."

He hunched forward. The passage through the narrows was only twice the width of the canoe. Craggy rocks rose out of the water on either side. Steve knew there were others just below the surface.

The waves pitched the canoe into the narrow channel. Tina pulled in her paddle to avoid the rocks.

Halfway through, a gust of wind lashed the back of the canoe. Steve automatically thrust out his paddle. He pushed hard against one of the rocks and kept the boat from smashing into it. Tina used her paddle to move the canoe forward. A few seconds later, they had entered Moose Cove.

Steve steered the boat toward the nearest shore. As soon as they were close enough, he grabbed an overhanging tree branch. He pulled the canoe in and scrambled onto the bank. With one hand grasping the branch, he held out the other to Tina. She leaped out of the canoe. They tied its rope to a sturdy shrub, tramped several yards into the woods, and collapsed on the soaking wet ground. The trees and shrubs offered some shelter from the rain, but not much.

"We made it," Steve said, breathing hard.

There was another flash of lightning. Thunder rumbled. Steve balanced his flashlight on a low rock so it wouldn't shine in their eyes. Tina wrapped her arms around her shoulders.

"I'm lucky you showed up," she said. "I don't even want to think about being out there alone."

Another clap of thunder interrupted her. It sounded slightly more distant.

"I hope everyone else sleeps through this

storm," Steve said. "If they get up and find us gone, they'll worry."

"No joke," Tina said. "Remember when they sent a search party to find us?"

Steve laughed. "You mean the time we hiked up Mount Penacook? Luke wanted to show us that cave he'd found. Then the sun set, and we couldn't see the path anymore."

"No more solo climbs that summer," Tina said.

She and Steve fell silent. They watched the rain form little pools of water on the rocks. After a few minutes, Tina looked at Steve.

"This is our last adventure together on Lost Lake," she said. "I'm glad it happened."

Steve opened his mouth to say something, but Tina had turned her head away.

Chapter Eleven

Joe put down his dad's journal and switched off his flashlight. It was dawn. He rubbed Wishbone's head.

"Ah, right between the ears," the terrier said. "You really know what you're doing."

Joe yawned. "I just remembered something from *Tom Sawyer, Detective*. Tom and Huck couldn't sleep one night. They were too worried about Uncle Silas and about Jubiter Dunlap's murder. So they decided to go outside at dawn and snoop around."

Wishbone lifted his head. "An excellent tactic. When in doubt, Super Sleuth *always* snoops!"

He jumped off the bed and walked to the door. Joe pulled on some jeans and a sweatshirt and followed. Outside the cabin, Wishbone paused for a moment. The light filtering through the trees was a pale, soft gray. The woods were silent.

Joe started up the path to the main cabin. Wishbone trotted alongside him, sniffing.

"Hmm, I recognize that scent. It's mine. Yep, there it is again. Ah, wonderful! The woods are starting to smell like home."

When they reached the clearing around the main cabin, Wishbone stopped and tilted his head to the side.

"I sense something," he barked. "A presence. . . . Yes! Over there!"

Joe's glance quickly followed Wishbone's. To the left of the cabin, at the edge of the woods, stood a tall, slim woman with short hair.

"Mrs. Joplin?" Joe said. He raised a hand to wave, but Ally's mother turned away. She walked into the woods and disappeared from view.

"That was strange," Joe murmured. He sat down on the porch steps. "Do you think she went for an early walk and took the wrong path?"

Wishbone rested his muzzle on Joe's knee. "Then why didn't she say hello?"

"Maybe she was curious to see our camp," Joe continued. "Maybe she was checking to make sure you weren't bothering the loons. But . . . why didn't she say hello?"

Wishbone sighed. "Didn't I just say that? No one ever listens to the dog."

"Lots of tourists in town," Wishbone commented, later that morning. He trotted at the heels of Joe and David as the boys hurried across the main square in Woodwich.

They had decided to canoe into town so they could check out the spot where Pat McKenzie's motorcycle had been stolen. Joe carried a map of Woodwich. On it, Luke had marked Timber Lane, where Pat's friend Gerry Rich lived.

Wishbone trotted past a few dozen pairs of feet in hiking shoes, sneakers, and sandals. Some stopped in front of the craft's shop. Others stepped into the little store that sold postcards and camera film. Every chair at the outdoor café was taken.

Wishbone and his friends didn't stop. They continued to the outskirts of town. There they found Timber Lane, a narrow, isolated road. They followed it for several minutes. On the left side of the road lay a grassy meadow. On the right were thick woods. Finally they came to a driveway on the right and a roadside mailbox.

"'Rich,'" Joe said, reading the large blue letters on the box.

They walked up the driveway. Wishbone saw a comfortable-looking old house in front of them. He noticed a little shed farther back.

"No cars around," David said.

Wishbone sniffed. "No dogs around, either."

"That's probably the tool shed," Joe said, pointing. "Pat said he left his motorcycle behind it."

Wishbone bounded toward the shed. "Super Sleuth is on the case."

Joe and David followed him.

"It doesn't look like anyone's home," David said, staring at the house. "There're no lights on."

They all began inspecting patches of grass and dirt around the shed.

"Look. The grass here is flattened," Joe said. He pointed to a spot in back of the shed. "This could be where Pat left his motorcycle. But that doesn't tell us much. I don't see tire marks leading in any particular direction."

"It looks like the shed gets a lot of use. There're footprints and tire tracks everywhere," David said.

"Sniffing is more useful than looking. Believe me," Wishbone said. "The nose knows!" He put his nose to the ground and inched forward, sniffing carefully. He slowly worked his way around the shed.

"Hey!" Wishbone started to bark. "I'm picking up a scent . . . "

Joe and David ran over to him. "I don't see any—"

A door slammed. Joe and David jumped at the sound. Wishbone's head whipped around to look at the house. A woman wearing overalls was walking toward them. She was frowning.

"What are you kids doing here?" she asked. "This is private property."

"You guys deal with the homeowner," Wishbone said. "I'm working on a major scent over here."

Joe faced the woman and said, "We're guests of Luke Talbot on Moose Cove. His canoe was vandalized in Woodwich two days ago. Last night Pat McKenzie told us his motorcycle was stolen from here. We're trying to figure out if there's some connection. Sorry we didn't knock first. We didn't think anyone was home."

"I heard about that canoe," the woman said. Her frown faded. "I'm Mrs. Rich, Gerry's mother."

While the boys introduced themselves, Wishbone continued to follow the scent he'd picked up.

"I certainly want to get to the bottom of this motorcycle business," he heard Mrs. Rich say. "So look around if you like. But I doubt you'll find anything. We searched this place with a fine-toothed comb yesterday." She nodded at Wishbone. "Seems like your dog is onto something. He probably smells a rabbit or a squirrel."

Wishbone kept his muzzle pointed toward the woods. "I beg to differ. Super Sleuth knows a human scent when he smells one." He barked once and bounded into the brush.

"Wishbone!" Joe shouted.

Wishbone was panting with excitement. He heard Joe and David plunge into the woods behind him. They were calling to him, but he didn't slow down.

I've smelled this scent before. But I can't pin down whom it belongs to.

Wishbone scrambled over rocks. He pushed past brambles. Now and then, he noticed snapped-off branches and crushed leaves.

"This is definitely a trail of some kind." He barked several times. "Come on, Joe and David! Hurry!"

He jumped over a tiny stream. It was no more than a trickle of water. But the ground around it was soft and damp.

"Hey, look at that!"

Wishbone came to a sudden stop. He sniffed at something in the moist dirt. "A tire track!"

He looked ahead, trying to follow the track. That was when he saw it—a bit of color about thirty feet away. A very unnatural-looking bright blue.

"What's that?"

Wishbone leaped forward. He quickly came

to a thick tangle of fallen trees and dead branches. The branches were heaped on top of something—something big and bright blue.

Wishbone sniffed the blue stuff. "Smells like plastic." He barked loudly. "Speed it up, guys!"

He grabbed a piece of the blue stuff with his teeth. He tried pulling, but he couldn't get a good grip.

"It's about time you two showed up." Wishbone dropped the blue plastic as Joe and David appeared.

"Looks like Wishbone's run into something," David said.

"This was no accident," Wishbone insisted. "Super Sleuth used all his powers to track this down."

"It's a tarp," Joe said, examining the blue plastic. "One of those big waterproof sheets that you use to protect things from the rain."

"It looks like someone tried to hide it with these branches," David added.

He and Joe began pulling away the branches. As soon as they had cleared off part of the tarp, they lifted it up.

Under the tarp stood a large motorcycle. Wishbone sniffed at its sparkling, dark red panels. "This belongs to Pat McKenzie."

"Good dog!" Joe bent down and rubbed Wishbone's head and back.

Wishbone wagged his tail. "All in a day's work for Super Sleuth."

"Why would a thief leave a valuable motorcycle here?" David wondered.

Joe thought for a moment. "Actually it makes sense. The bike was stolen during the day. There was no way of getting it out of town without someone recognizing it. Woodwich is a small place. Everyone knows everyone else."

"I guess the thief is waiting to wheel the bike out of the woods at night. Waiting a few days or even a week would make sense. No one would think to look back here."

Joe nodded. "We've got to report this to the sheriff right away."

The boys pulled the tarp back down and replaced the branches. They began retracing their steps out of the woods, moving as fast as they could. Wishbone had less trouble slipping between branches and avoiding brambles.

"Ouch!" Joe said.

Wishbone stopped to see what had happened.

Joe stood next to a tall, barbed shrub. He was rubbing a scratch on his wrist. A long thorn had snagged the sleeve of his T-shirt. As Joe worked the material free, Wishbone noticed a small scrap of blue caught on another thorn. Just as he was about to call out his discovery, Joe noticed it, too.

"Hey, a piece of denim." Joe pulled it off the shrub. "Whoever hid Pat's motorcycle back here must have gotten caught on this bush, too," he said. He put the scrap of material into his jeans pocket and hurried on.

About twenty minutes later, the boys and Wishbone reached the town square. From a half-block away, Joe saw Sheriff Eastwood step out of his office.

"Sheriff Eastwood!" Joe called out.

He dashed down the street. David and Wishbone followed him. The sheriff locked the door and walked toward a van parked at the curb. He looked up as Joe and David stopped in front of him, breathing hard.

"We found Pat McKenzie's motorcycle," Joe said.

The sheriff's eyes opened wide. He listened silently while Joe and David explained what had happened. When they were done, Sheriff Eastwood looked at his watch and said, "I'll skip lunch. I want to get that motorcycle right away—before anything else happens. Then I'll notify the McKenzies." He nodded at the boys and Wishbone. "Thanks. You make an impressive trio."

The sheriff jumped into his van. As he started the motor, he leaned his head out of the window. "Give that dog a nice reward. He deserves it!"

Wishbone wagged his tail and stood tall on his four legs. It was as if he were trying to say, "I couldn't agree more!"

"Want to go to the café?" David asked Joe. "I'm starving."

"Me, too," Joe said.

They walked down the street. As they neared the café, Joe noticed that all the outdoor tables were taken. Then a couple stood up, left a tip for their waiter, and departed.

"Perfect timing," Joe moved quickly through the crowded café and sat down at the free table. David sat down across from him. Wishbone lagged behind. Joe noticed that he was eagerly sniffing the air near the next table.

"Those sandwich scraps aren't for you, buddy," Joe said, laughing.

He glanced at the two people there. They both wore hats and sunglasses. One was reading a book. The other held a copy of the *Woodwich Weekly* in front of her face. A moment later, Joe recognized them.

"Ally, Mrs. Joplin," Joe said. "Hi!"

Ally and her mother looked up. They both smiled and said hello. Ally leaned over and rubbed Wishbone's head.

"Did you come into town by boat?" David asked.

"By canoe," Mrs. Joplin said. She laid her newspaper on the table. "It's the nicest way to go anywhere on the lake. How about you?"

As David answered, Joe looked more closely at Mrs. Joplin's newspaper. He noticed that something on the open page was circled in red. It was the announcement of the next day's auction.

Mrs. Joplin quickly refolded the newspaper. Glancing at Joe out of the corner of her eye, she shoved the paper into her large tote bag and stood up.

"Let's get going, Ally," she said. "I'm not sure the weather's going to hold. I heard someone mention rain."

Why is she in such a hurry all of a sudden? Joe wondered.

His thoughts were interrupted by the waiter, who came over with menus. While Mrs. Joplin paid the check, Ally gathered up her things. She picked up a sheet of paper that was lying on the table. Joe saw it only for a second. Then Ally put it into her backpack, along with her book.

"Catch you later," she said to the boys. She and her mother walked away.

Joe's mind was racing. "Did you see Mrs. Joplin's newspaper?" he whispered.

David nodded. "The auction announcement was circled in red."

"That's not all. Did you see what Ally put into her backpack?" Joe didn't wait for David to answer. "It was your sheet of questions and information. The paper you had at the Tucker camp yesterday."

Joe took a deep breath. "Ally must be the one who took it out of your jacket pocket!"

Chapter Twelve

"Wow," David said. By the look on his face, Joe could tell how surprised David was.

"Ally must have gone back to the Tucker camp," Joe said, piecing it together. "She must have found your jacket before you did."

"But why did she take the paper?" David wondered. "Do you think her mom is planning to bid at the auction? We wrote about how Luke and the Castles are bidding. And about how finding the Talbot watch could help Luke make the highest bid. That information could be useful to another bidder."

"Definitely," Joe said. He frowned. "If Mrs. Joplin is bidding on the Tucker camp, that's bad news for Luke."

He looked up as the waiter came to take their order.

Fifteen minutes later, the waiter brought their sandwiches. "Let's eat fast," Joe said to

David. "I want to tell Luke about the Joplins." He glanced at the sky. He could still see patches of blue, but the clouds were growing thicker. "I hope it doesn't rain."

The boys gulped down their food and paid their check. They hurried to the town dock with Wishbone at their heels.

The terrier seemed to understand that they were in a rush. He jumped into the canoe while Joe and David grabbed the paddles. Joe, sitting in back, steered the boat toward the five boulders. The wind had picked up, making the water choppy. Joe saw David glance at the sky.

"We'd better paddle faster," David said over his shoulder. "I just felt a drop of rain."

Joe pulled his paddle through the choppy water even harder. He could see David straining. Wishbone was sitting tall in the middle of the canoe with his ears pricked up.

As they glided past the five boulders, the drops of rain turned into a steady patter. The patter turned into heavy rain. By the time the boat reached the middle of the main lake, it was pouring. The wind blew in hard gusts.

Joe shook the water off his face. He wiped his eyes with the sleeve of his jacket. He could barely make out the rocky narrows ahead at the entrance to Moose Cove. He thought of his father. He pictured Steve Talbot trying to keep his canoe on course in the storm. He could almost hear his father's voice. *Stroke, back. Stroke, back. Harder . . . harder!*

The distance between their canoe and the rocky narrows shrank steadily. Yet the wind was blowing even harder. Waves rose up like huge ridges topped with foam. The canoe rose with them like a scrap of bark. Up . . . down . . . up . . .

"We're going to get swamped!" David shouted over his shoulder.

As he spoke, the canoe dropped behind one wave. The next was about to peak.

"Wishbone!" Joe yelled.

The wave splashed over the side of the canoe. It knocked the terrier over and started to sweep him overboard.

"No!" Joe lunged forward and grabbed one paw. He lost hold of his paddle. It flipped over and slid into the water. David reached out and just barely managed to grab it. The canoe tilted . . .

The next few seconds vanished in a shower of spray. Joe pulled Wishbone back into the canoe. He looked at the terrier to make sure he was okay. "Under the seat you go, boy," Joe said.

David held out Joe's paddle. Grabbing it, Joe remembered his father's journal.

"We've got to head right into the waves!" he shouted.

Somehow, he and David managed to turn the canoe ninety degrees. It met the waves head on. *Slam!* . . . *Slam!* . . . *Slam!* The canoe bumped and lurched. But the waves didn't flood it.

As they neared the narrows, David called out, "Rocks below us! Watch your paddle."

Joe could feel his muscles strain to hold his paddle firm against the swirling water. He hunched forward and steered the boat into the tight passage between the craggy rocks. The waves pushed them sideways, to the right. David pulled in his paddle to avoid the rocks just below the surface. The canoe lurched toward the rock on their right. Both Joe and David thrust their paddles against it. Joe gritted his teeth as they pushed the canoe away from the looming rock.

And then the canoe passed through the narrows.

Joe pushed his streaming hair off his forehead. His waterlogged jacket and jeans felt heavy on his limbs. He heard a low rumble.

"Thunder," David said. "Should we head for the shore right here?"

Joe checked to make sure Wishbone was still safe under the canoe seat. Then he looked for the Talbot dock across Moose Cove. He made a rapid calculation. "That thunder was pretty far away," he said. "I think we can make it to the dock."

"Let's go for it!" David sent the canoe forward with a powerful stroke.

The rain didn't let up. The wind, however,

wasn't quite as strong as it had been on the main lake. A few minutes later, they neared the dock. David leaned forward and grabbed the edge of it. He pulled the canoe in.

"We made it!" he said. He scrambled onto the dock.

Just as Joe stepped onto the dock, lightning flashed. A few seconds later, a clap of thunder seemed to rip apart the atmosphere.

"Not a minute to spare," Joe said.

He lifted Wishbone out of the canoe. David began hauling the boat out of the water. The boys turned it bottom up so it would stay dry inside.

Lightning flashed again as they dashed along the path to the main cabin. They splashed up the steps and across the porch.

"I hope Luke is home." Joe pulled open the door. "I want to tell him about Mrs. Joplin bidding at the auction." He stamped his muddy sneakers on the mat inside the door.

Joe he looked up and his eyes rested on a yellow hooded jacket.

Ethan Castle was wearing it. He stood in the middle of the main room of the cabin. His blond hair was damp and matted down. He stared hard at Joe.

Uh-oh, Joe thought as David and Wishbone stepped inside next to him. *He heard what I said about Mrs. Joplin.*

Luke was bent over the fireplace, adding a log to the fire. He turned around and said, "You guys are soaking wet. You'd better take off your shoes and socks. I'll find some dry towels. Then you can warm up by the fire."

He went into the bedroom. Joe and David said hello to Ethan. As they pulled off their shoes and socks, Joe noticed that Ethan continued staring at David and him.

"What were you saying about Mrs. Joplin and the auction?" Ethan began.

Returning to the room, Luke interrupted him. "I've laid out a pile of dry towels and some dry clothes. A little big, but they'll do until you can get out back to the other cabin," he told Joe and David. "We can hang your wet things in front of the fire."

Joe was glad to escape Ethan's question. But when he and David walked back into the main room in dry clothes, Ethan picked up where he had left off.

"What did I hear you say about this Mrs. Joplin?" Ethan asked again. "She's bidding on the Tucker property tomorrow?"

Joe reminded himself to observe Ethan carefully. "Well, it's just a guess," he replied as he and David draped their wet things on chairs near the fire. "We saw her and her daughter at the café in Woodwich. Mrs. Joplin had a copy of the *Woodwich Weekly*. I noticed that the announcement of the auction was circled in red."

He decided not to mention seeing Ally with their missing sheet of questions.

"Mrs. Joplin could have picked up someone else's paper," Luke said, shrugging. "Or she might just be interested in seeing the auction. A lot of folks will show up to watch."

"Quite right." Ethan cut off the discussion with an impatient shake of his head. "Let's get back to business," he said to Luke. "As I was saying before, it makes no sense for you to bid tomorrow."

Luke calmly returned Ethan's gaze. "I think that's my business."

"Let's be frank," Ethan said. His voice had a sharp edge. "I have a lot more money than you do. I'll end up outbidding you. All you'll do is drive up the price."

Luke's voice remained mild, even relaxed. "It's a matter of principle for me. I think you know that, Ethan. I love the peace and quiet of Lost Lake. I don't like motorboats or waterskiing. I—"

"You don't understand development," Ethan cut in. His face turned red. "You're living in the past!"

"Let's just say we disagree on the subject," Luke said. "You'll act on your beliefs and desires. And I'll act on mine."

"I knew this would be a waste of time," Ethan muttered.

He zipped up his jacket and walked straight to the door. Opening it, he turned and glared at Luke.

"I've been waiting for lakefront property for years," he said. "I don't plan on losing this opportunity. Tomorrow the Tucker place is going to be mine!"

Chapter Thirteen

The door shut with a bang.

Wishbone listened as Ethan crossed the porch and walked around to the back of the cabin. A few seconds later, his jeep's motor started up, and he drove off.

"That fellow has the charm of a wet alley cat." Wishbone shook his own wet fur. He settled in front of the fire next to Joe.

"He's pretty confident about the auction," David said.

Luke stood up and poked the fire. "He has reason to be. His reason is money."

Wishbone saw the worry in Luke's gray eyes. He seemed to try to shake himself free of it. "What else did you do in town today?" Luke asked.

Wishbone turned to Joe. "Tell him the big news!"

"We found Pat MacKenzie's motorcycle,"

Joe and David said together.

"You what?" A surprised smile flashed across Luke's face.

"Well, actually, Wishbone found it," Joe added.

"Thanks, Joe." Wishbone lifted his head, letting the heat from the fire warm him. "Super Sleuth appreciates exact wording."

He listened while the boys described how they had discovered the motorcycle in the woods and reported it to the sheriff. They also told Luke the *complete* story about what had happened in the café in Woodwich.

"It was pretty strange," Joe said. "As soon as I noticed Mrs. Joplin's newspaper, she put it away and got up to leave. Then I saw that Ally had David's missing information sheet."

"I bet they're planning to bid on the Tucker camp," David said. "And now Ethan knows it. If the Castles are trying to knock bidders out of the auction—"

"They might try to scare off Mrs. Joplin," Joe finished.

Luke nodded. "But they don't have much time."

"They could try something tonight," David suggested.

"I'm going to be gone most of the night," Luke said. "If you boys decide to do any investigating, watch yourselves. Someone wants the

Tucker property really badly. Badly enough to cause some serious property damage. I've got to get over to Ashton for the Regional Lakes Association meeting. It's a two-hour drive, so I won't be back until after midnight. You're on your own for dinner. But there's lots of stuff in the fridge."

He glanced out the large front window. "It's stopped raining. I'll leave the McKenzies' and the sheriff's number by the phone."

"We'll be fine," Joe said.

"I'm going down to our cabin," David said. "I want to update the case files on the computer."

"I'll go with you," Joe said.

"Wait for the dog!" Wishbone rose up on all fours. He followed as the boys left the cabin.

"We should stake out the Joplins' camp tonight," Joe was saying.

"In case the Castles try something?" David asked.

Joe nodded. "I was thinking about that scene in *Tom Sawyer, Detective*. Remember when Tom and Hank watched what turned out to be the murder? They hid near the woods and saw everything."

Wishbone stared into the dark woods late that night. The ground was damp and cold. Wishbone shivered, causing the metal tag on his collar to jangle.

"Sh-sh," Joe whispered, steadying Wishbone with his hand.

David pressed a tiny button on his watch. The dial lit up. "It's almost midnight," he whispered to Joe.

About thirty feet in front of them stood the little house where the Joplins were staying. The living-room light was still on.

The boys had wrapped themselves in wool blankets. Two flashlights, a half-empty thermos of cocoa, and several candy-bar wrappers lay in a neat pile next to them.

Joe rested his chin on his knees. Wishbone knew how worried he was. The missing watch, the vandalized canoe, the stolen motorcycle—everything was still a mystery.

And the auction is in just fourteen hours! Wishbone thought. *Still, fourteen hours are fourteen opportunities for Super Sleuth. I'll—*

His ears pricked up. His whiskers quivered.

"A noise. Far away in the woods. Near the lake . . . There it is again. That's near the shore, all right. *Too* near!"

Wishbone jumped up. In four leaps he reached the clearing around the house.

"Wishbone!" Joe kept his voice low. "Come back!"

"Don't worry, buddy. I'm following up on a lead." Wishbone raced on. "I won't disturb your stakeout."

Three seconds more, and he reached the path that led down to the lake. He ran as fast as he could in the dark. As he neared the water, alarm bells went off inside his head.

There it is! The dreaded scent. Raccoons!

Keeping his head low, Wishbone made a rapid turn to the right. The path continued along the shore, in the direction of the spit of land where the loon nest was. The scent of raccoons grew stronger and stronger. Wishbone's heart pounded as he ran faster.

"*En garde,* you masked bandits! It's the knight in shining fur!"

He heard scrambling noises near the water just ahead. Out of the corner of his eye, he saw a human figure. It lunged toward him. It was Mrs. Joplin!

"Stop!" she cried. "You can't go near the loon nest!"

Wishbone felt her fingertips on his flanks. "Don't stop me!" he shouted, trying to spring forward. Using all his strength, he pulled free of her grasp. "Yes!"

Moonlight glowed over the lake. Wishbone could see the spit of land. It was just up ahead. Two large, dark forms were moving toward the loon nest. The raccoons!

Barking as loud as he could, Wishbone leaped forward. He reached the spit of land.

Aa-o-aa-o-aa-o-aa! A loon screeched.

Splash! The nesting bird threw itself into the water.

Wishbone hurled himself at the raccoons. They sprang off the spit of land. They, too, splashed in the shallow water. Then they scrambled ashore and dashed into the woods.

Aa-o-aa-o-aa-o-aa! The loon screeched again.

"Sorry you had such a scare." Wishbone stopped, gasping for breath. "But you're safe now."

Still panting, the terrier began to back off the spit of land. The sooner he moved away from the nest, the sooner the loon would return to it. Reaching the shore, he turned—and stopped short.

Mrs. Joplin loomed over him.

"Uh-oh," Wishbone said.

"Good dog! Good Wishbone! You scared away those raccoons." Mrs. Joplin kneeled down and scratched Wishbone behind his ears. "You are so smart and brave."

"You finally noticed," Wishbone said. He sat down and wagged his tail.

"You deserve a big reward," Mrs. Joplin went on.

"Very true."

"I'm going to take you home and get you something good to eat."

Wishbone gazed up at her. "I know you've been acting strange about the auction. But you're an animal lover. I believe animal lovers have good hearts. Especially if they give out food."

Just then, he heard voices and running footsteps on the path.

"Wishbone!" a very familiar voice called.

"Joe!" Wishbone turned toward the voice. A few seconds later, Joe and David appeared. Ally Joplin was close behind them. They all had flashlights.

"What happened?" Joe asked breathlessly.

"Your fine dog just saved the loon eggs," Mrs. Joplin said. "I was sitting near the water when I heard a terrible racket. Wishbone scared off two raccoons in the nick of time."

Joe, David, and Ally all began praising Wishbone. "'Atta boy . . . You're a hero . . . What a great dog . . . You're the best."

Wishbone sighed with pleasure. "No need to stop."

"We should put some fencing around the spit of land," Ally said. "That would keep the raccoons away."

"Good idea," her mother said. "We can do it first thing in the morning. But right now, how about a midnight snack? I was going to take Wishbone up to our house for a reward."

At the word *reward*, Wishbone's tail wagged faster. "Lead the way!"

They all started walking along the shore-line path. Wishbone was thinking about his reward.

Sausage pizza? Probably not this late. Roast beef on rye? Maybe. Smoked . . . smoked . . .

Wishbone stopped in his tracks and sniffed. "Hey, I smell smoke! Yes, that's definitely smoke. The breeze is carrying it from the direction of . . . the Talbot cabin!"

He barked the alarm as he ran full-speed in the direction of the Talbot camp. "Come on, everyone! There's something burning!"

Wishbone could hear the others' voices and footsteps behind him. But he didn't stop.

At the Talbot dock, he made a sharp left turn. He dashed up the path that led to the main cabin. The smell of smoke was growing stronger. It made his nose twitch.

"Something's burning!" he heard Joe shout.

Wishbone raced into the clearing around the cabin and stopped short. Smoke poured out of the woodshed attached to the side of the cabin. Under the shed roof, flames leaped from the tall pile of logs.

Wishbone threw back his head and howled.

"Fire!"

Chapter Fourteen

Joe felt his heart begin to pound when he saw flames shooting from the woodshed. He was breathing hard. Behind him, David, Ally, and Mrs. Joplin began to cough.

"There's a fire extinguisher inside the cabin!" Joe yelled. "Near the stove."

He turned toward the porch, but David was closer. He bolted up the stairs. Ally was right behind him.

"There's a hose in back," Mrs. Joplin shouted. She started running around the side of the cabin.

Joe sprinted after her. Turning the corner, he saw a water pipe attached to the back wall. A hose was coiled on the ground nearby.

"Turn the water on all the way," he called to Mrs. Joplin. "I'll get the hose."

It wasn't until he bent down to grab the hose that a question occurred to Joe. *How did she know this was back here?*

Joe glanced up—and froze. In the woods behind the cabin stood a human figure. The person was half-hidden by the trees. But Joe got a clear look at what he or she was wearing.

A yellow hooded jacket.

Joe stared. He saw the person rub one foot against the other leg. Then the figure turned and disappeared deeper into the woods.

The image of the yellow-hooded figure was still in Joe's mind as he seized the brass nozzle. Water began gushing out of it. Hauling the long hose behind him, he rushed toward the wood-shed. Every time he breathed in, the swirling smoke stung his lungs.

David was already there. He aimed the fire extinguisher at some high flames.

Whoosh! A white mist covered the flames. They sank down.

Joe pointed the hose at the side of the shed attached to the cabin. The wood boards crackled and sizzled under the stream of water. Smoke and steam billowed up. The flames sputtered. Joe quickly soaked the side of the cabin to protect it from the fire. Swinging the hose to the left, he aimed the water at the middle of the shed. Out of the corner of his eye he saw Ally appear, carrying a large pail of water.

"I'll help you!" Mrs Joplin called out to her. The two of them aimed the pail of water at

146

the worst part of the blaze. They drenched it. Joe followed with more water. He and David moved quickly from one spot to another. The flames hissed as they went out. They sent up large clouds of steam and smoke.

Wishbone ran up and down the clearing, sniffing the smoke-filled air.

Just as the boys were smothering the last flames, Joe heard a car on the dirt road. Headlights beamed through the smoky haze. The car stopped in back of the cabin. A door slammed, and then Joe heard running footsteps.

"What in the world—"

Joe could barely see Luke Talbot's face in the dark. But he could hear the shock in his voice.

"Someone set the woodshed on fire," Joe explained. He coughed and wiped the sweat off his face with his sleeve. "We were all down by the lake when Wishbone smelled the smoke. We got here just in time."

"I don't think there's any damage to the cabin," David added.

He picked up his flashlight and shone it on the side of the cabin. The fire had left only scorch marks and smoke streaks. Luke examined the half-burnt woodshed. "Looks like the fire is completely out. Nice work, boys."

Luke coughed as he glanced around the dark clearing. "Oh," he said. "I didn't realize anyone else was here."

"Hi. I'm Ally Joplin." Ally stepped forward from beside the woodshed.

"And I'm Mrs. Joplin, Ally's mom." Mrs. Joplin's voice came from the porch steps.

"We're staying at the next camp," Ally added.

"Well, a fire isn't much of a welcome to the Talbot camp," Luke said, coughing. "But welcome anyway. Let's go inside, and I'll make some cocoa or tea. I want to thank you all—and Wishbone—for saving the cabin. I'd also like to hear exactly what happened."

Luke started for the porch stairs. Joe noticed that Ally and her mom held back.

"It's pretty late . . ." Mrs. Joplin started to say.

"It'll only take a minute to make something to drink," Luke insisted.

Everyone followed Luke into the cabin. Mrs. Joplin entered the room last. Joe found himself watching her closely. Something was bothering him—something he couldn't figure out.

Luke put a box of cocoa and five mugs on the kitchen counter. While he got milk from the refrigerator, David got out a large saucepan. Mrs. Joplin picked up the cocoa box. Keeping her back to the room, she read the directions printed on the label. She held the box close to her face. Joe couldn't take his eyes off her.

"That's it!" Joe suddenly said.

Everyone turned and looked at him. Wishbone's ears pricked up.

"I know who you are," Joe said to Mrs. Joplin. "You're Tina Tucker!"

The room became so quiet that Joe could hear the leaves rustling outside. Mrs. Joplin looked startled at first. But then her face relaxed.

"You're right. I *am* Tina Tucker," she said. Her voice sounded almost relieved. "But I use my husband's last name now. Joplin." She turned to Luke and smiled. "Hello, Luke. It's been a long time."

"Wow," was all Luke said at first. Then he laughed and threw his arms around Tina in a big hug.

"This is mind-boggling," Luke said. "I have a thousand questions to ask you. I don't know where to begin," Luke said. "Well, let's start with, 'Why the big mystery about your identity?'"

"I'll explain later," Tina said.

"All right, then, how about, 'When did you cut that long hair?'"

Tina chuckled. "Oh, probably the same time you stopped wearing your bandana."

She held out her hand to Ally. "This is my oldest daughter. She has two younger sisters at home."

Turning to Joe, Tina said, "Ally told me your name is Joe Talbot. Are you Luke's son?"

"Actually, I'm Steve Talbot's son."

"Steve's son! Yes, of course. I can see a resemblance," Tina said. "How wonderful! Is he here, too?"

Joe shook his head. "My dad died eight years ago."

Tina breathed in slowly. Her eyes filled with tears. "I'm so sorry," she whispered. "So very sorry."

No one spoke for a minute or so. Finally, Luke said, "We have a lot of catching up to do. Years and years. But there's one thing I've got to know right away. Joe, how did you figure out Tina's identity?"

Joe didn't miss the grin David shot at him.

"I bet you noticed a detail," David said. "Like a gesture. Tom Sawyer's method."

Joe nodded. "I noticed that Mrs. Joplin held the cocoa box close to her face to read the label. She did the same thing when she read the newspaper in the café. That reminded me of a picture of Tina, Luke, my dad, and Mac on the dock here. Tina had a book, and she held it the same way."

"That was enough to figure it out?" Tina asked.

"No," Joe replied. "But then everything else fell into place. You circled the newspaper announcement of the Tucker camp auction. You were really concerned about the loons. Luke told us that Tina Tucker's grandfather founded the Loon Protection Society. And if you were Tina, you'd know the Talbot cabin. That would explain how you knew where Luke keeps the water hose."

Wishbone barked up at Joe, his tail wagging. Joe almost had the impression he was saying, "Good job, buddy!"

"You sound just like your dad," Tina said to Joe. "He always figured out mystery stories before he finished reading the books." Smiling, she said to Luke, "Remember the youth sleuth of Lost Lake?"

While Luke made the cocoa, Tina explained why she had returned to Lost Lake.

"We're very happy living in Vancouver," she said. "But my greatest dream has always been to have a summer place here. So for the last few years, I've been in touch with a real estate agent in Woodwich."

"That's how you found out about the auction?" Joe asked.

Tina nodded. "I knew I had to bid on our old property. And I wanted Ally to come with me. I was just her age when my family left the lake. My hope was to buy the Tucker camp and then surprise my old friends. That's why I didn't tell you I was here, Luke." She paused and added, "I suppose it's all just a dream. I don't have a great deal of money."

Luke's eyes met Tina's. "I don't either," he said. "But . . . well, why can't we bid together? I want to save the property from more development. And I can't think of a better way than having the Tuckers back." He looked hopeful. "A joint bid would be twice as strong."

"Mom, that's a fantastic idea!" Ally said.

Tina looked back and forth between her daughter and Luke. She grinned and said, "Let's do it, Luke."

There was a feeling of celebration as they all sat down at the table with their mugs. Joe put a slice of turkey in a bowl for Wishbone. As the terrier gobbled it up, Joe looked across the table at Ally and her mother. "I guess you know that David and I are trying to figure out what happened to the Talbot family watch," he said.

Ally's cheeks turned red. "We know," she said. "Because of that sheet of paper I took out of David's jacket pocket. It was an awful thing to do. But I saw you digging near the old Tucker cabin. I went back later to try to find out why. That's when I saw David's jacket. There was information about the auction on the paper and . . ." She stared down into her cocoa mug. "I'm really sorry."

"But you'd been digging in that spot yourself before that, right?" Joe asked Ally and her mother. "We saw that the dirt had already been disturbed."

Tina nodded. "The day I left Lost Lake, I buried a sort of treasure box there. It was filled with little things that were important to me. You know—loon feathers, a swimming prize, a stone from the top of Mount Penacook. I promised myself that I'd come back to Lost Lake some day and get them."

"I grew up hearing about that box," Ally continued the story. "So my mom and I dug it up together." She leaned forward. "Why were you guys digging there?"

"Because Sheriff Eastwood told us about Tina burying something the day she left," David explained. "We thought it might have something to do with—"

Tina Tucker finished his sentence. "The missing watch." She fell silent.

Joe took a deep breath. The question on his mind was a hard one to ask. But he had to. "Mrs. Joplin, did you take the Talbot watch?"

Tina's eyes moved from Joe to David to Ally to Luke.

"Yes, I did," she said quietly.

Chapter Fifteen

Every pair of eyes in the room turned to Tina. A tense silence hung in the air. Wishbone sat straight up, his whiskers twitching.

"How did Joe—" Luke began.

Before he said another word, Joe got up from the table. He took one of the camp logs down from the shelf. Flipping through the pages, he said, "I read something the other night that stuck in my mind. Gram Talbot wrote it the day the Tuckers left Lost Lake. Here it is."

Joe read from the log. "'Poor Tina is so upset. She's not acting like herself.'"

"Let me tell you what really happened," Tina said. She squeezed her daughter's hand. "Ally already knows."

As Tina began to speak, she didn't look at anyone in the room. She seemed to be looking into the past.

"We spent the day before we left Lost Lake packing. It was the saddest day of my life . . .

Real time faded away for Joe, just the way it did when he read his dad's journal. Tina's words took shape in his mind like a scene in a movie.

Fourteen-year-old Tina stared at the bedroom that had always been hers at Lost Lake. It didn't look like her room anymore. Gone were the yellow curtains she had chosen when she was ten. Gone were the blue print bedspread from India and the pressed leaf collection tacked to the walls. And the miniature canoe paddle from the Woodwich town fair. All gone. She had packed everything into the large carton that sat on the floor.

Tina threw the bead necklace she was holding onto the mattress. "Man," she muttered, "this is a total drag. I've got to get out of here for a while."

She stepped into the hallway. From there, she could see her mother and Gram Talbot packing dishes in the main room. Her eyes began to smart. She bit her lip to force back the tears. As she turned away, she heard someone shout in the distance. The sound traveled across the lake water.

"That sounds like my husband," Gram Talbot said to Tina's mother. "Maybe he's finally caught a good-sized bass."

Tina left the cabin through the back door. Looking down at the ground, she crossed the clearing to the woods. She walked slowly along the path to the Talbot camp. Her moccasins made a crunching sound on the dead leaves. The wide legs of her bell-bottomed jeans brushed against fallen branches.

If we just had more money, she thought. *We wouldn't be selling our camp. Money, money, money. I'm so sick of hearing about money problems!*

Tina snatched a twig that she had brushed past and broke it off. The rough bark left a pink scratch on the palm of her hand. Her head ached.

Minutes later she came to the clearing behind the Talbot camp. Tina glanced around for Joe and Luke.

Maybe they're inside.

As Tina opened the back door, the front screen door slammed. She saw Luke dash across the front porch and down the stairs. He was carrying a camera.

Tina walked down the little hallway and stopped.

"Anybody home?" she called. When no one answered, she looked into Pops and Gram

Talbot's bedroom. Something there sparkled and caught her eye.

The watch. The diamond watch. She stepped over to the desk and picked it up. She had seen the watch so many other times. The smooth gold case felt like satin in the palm of her hand. The diamonds flashed blue and green light. The watch felt heavy . . . and very valuable. She stood there. Time seemed to stop.

Tina turned and walked to the door in three slow steps. As she moved, she slid the watch into her jeans pocket. It felt even heavier. As she slipped out the back door, she heard noise at the front of the cabin. Someone was running up the porch steps. Tina's heart began pounding. She walked away from the cabin quickly and entered the woods. Then she moved along the path, walking fast, then running.

Halfway to the Tucker camp, she stopped. She bent over, trying to catch her breath. She felt dizzy.

What am I doing? This is crazy. I've got the Talbot family watch in my pocket! Tina turned around and started walking back to the Talbot camp. Then she stopped again. *I can't go back while someone is there. It's too embarrassing. Why did I take it?* Tina's face flushed. Her knees wobbled.

She turned around and started walking slowly to the Tucker camp. *I'll return the watch tonight . . . when everyone's asleep.*

158

Tina's voice stopped. Joe looked up to see her place her hand on Luke's wrist.

"I *did* return the watch that night," she said. "Actually it was about one-thirty in the morning."

"Before you and my dad got caught out on the lake in that rainstorm," Joe put in.

Tina gave a surprised nod. "I found a tear in the screen on your grandparents' bedroom window. I slipped the watch through so it would land on the window-seat cushion. All these years I assumed your family had the watch. Then—"

"We read about the missing watch on David's sheet," Ally said to Luke. "My mom wanted to talk to you right away."

"I was here at dawn this morning," Tina went on. "I was waiting for everyone to get up. I saw Joe at the edge of the clearing. But then I decided to wait until after the auction."

"So the watch just . . . disappeared?" David frowned. "How could that happen?"

Luke took a deep breath, pressing Tina's hand. "Let's forget the watch for now. For me, the important thing is to have you back at Lost Lake. And to make it permanent at the auction tomorrow." He glanced at the clock. "Wow, it's after one in the morning. We still have to talk about our bid."

He paused for a moment. "Let's do this. Let's have breakfast here at nine-thirty. The auction's not until two. That gives us time to plan our strategy. And we'll call Sheriff Eastwood to report the fire. You folks will have to describe everything you saw."

Joe breathed in sharply. "The person in the yellow hooded jacket! I forgot until just now. I saw someone in the woods when I ran to the back of the cabin for the hose. The person was wearing a yellow hooded jacket. Whoever it was disappeared behind the trees. I was so busy with the fire, it slipped my mind."

"Was the jacket like the one we saw Ethan Castle wearing?" David asked.

"Yes. I didn't get a good look at the person's face. But the jacket was the same," Joe said.

Scowling, Luke stood up. "We'll have to tell the sheriff about that, too," he said. "Too bad we don't have proof that it was Ethan. That would certainly be enough to bar the Castles from the auction."

Ten minutes later, Joe, David, and Wishbone were in their cabin. David sat on his bed, his back against the wall, his hands behind his head. He grinned at Joe.

"Nice work tonight, Talbot. I'm impressed.

You reminded me of Tom Sawyer. Remember the big courtroom scene at the end? Tom suddenly reveals the real identity of the stranger in town. Everyone is amazed. Then he reveals what happened to the stolen diamonds, and everyone is even more amazed. You were just like that!"

"Thanks, Barnes," Joe said. He, too, was smiling. He was proud of his detective work. And he liked the way David called him by his last name. *That's what my dad and Luke used to do.*

David yawned and got under the blankets. "What a day! I can't believe it was just yesterday morning that we found Pat MacKenzie's motorcycle. It seems like a week ago." He yawned again. "I'm too tired to update the case files right now. I'll do it . . . first thing . . ." His voice trailed off and his eyes closed.

Joe stretched out on his bed with his dad's journal and *Tom Sawyer, Detective.* Wishbone hopped onto the bed and lay down next to him. Joe reached out to rub the terrier's head.

"I've solved more of the watch mystery than my father ever did," he said, keeping his voice low. But the watch is still missing. How could it disappear into thin air?"

He opened *Tom Sawyer, Detective* and turned to the courtroom scene. He chuckled as he reread Tom's wildly dramatic speeches. A few minutes later, he picked up his father's journal and began reading.

> **August 3. Gram searched for the watch again today. She thinks maybe Luke or I left it lying around without realizing it. It's no use. We took the whole cabin apart three days ago, after we first discovered the watch was missing. . . .**

"Hey, it's tipping over," Steve Talbot said to Luke. "We'd better lean this thing against the armchair."

The boys put down the mattress they were carrying and balanced it against a chair.

"That's it," Luke said. "The bedroom is cleared out."

Steve glanced around the main room of the cabin. The bedframe, dresser, desk, and lamps from the bedroom were all there. Gram had organized the search for the missing watch after she returned from the Tuckers' camp and heard the news. Now she stood at the desk, going through the drawers one by one.

"It's the best way to find something," she said, without looking up. "Clear out the room and turn everything inside-out."

Steve and Luke returned to the bedroom. Pops was on his hands and knees, examining the bare floor.

"These boards are a hundred years old," he said. "Some of them are loose and have big cracks. I'm going to pull up whatever's loose and make sure the watch didn't slip underneath."

"We'll help," Luke said. He grabbed a hammer and knelt down.

Steve walked over to the window seat. Gram had removed the cushion that always covered it. The seat was like a large box made of wood boards. It was nailed to the wall below the window.

"There's a space between the wall and the boards," Steve said. "Maybe the watch slipped down there."

Pops looked at the space. "Let's pry the seat farther away from the wall. Maybe we'll get lucky."

Using a large hammer, Steve went to work. He pulled back the seat and bent down to peer into the larger space.

Come on, watch, he thought. *Please be here!*

Luke looked over his shoulder. "Ugh. That's truly foul."

A hundred years of dust and grime filled the gap. The boys swept it out carefully and sifted through the dirt. They found coins, pencils, buttons, pins, and paper scraps.

"No watch," Luke said, sifting through the last of the dust.

Pops sighed. "You guys can nail the seat back into place," he said. "I'll finish working on the floor."

Steve could hear the disappointment in Pops voice. He felt his own hopes sink like a lead weight in the pit of his stomach.

I should have put the watch back inside the desk, he thought. *Why didn't I do it?* He swung his hammer hard against a nail.

Thwack!

Joe put down his dad's journal and turned out the light.

When he opened his eyes again, he was sure no more than a few minutes could have passed. Yet a shaft of sunlight made him squint. It was Friday morning.

Turning his head, he saw David sitting on the edge of the other bed. His computer was on his lap and he was tapping on the keyboard. Joe glanced at the clock on the dresser.

"Nine o'clock!" Suddenly he was wide-awake. He jumped out of bed and grabbed his swimsuit. "Just a half-hour before breakfast and auction planning. Have you gone for a swim yet?"

"Nope," David said. "I've been waiting for you." He tapped out a few computer commands and shut off the machine. "Let's do it."

Wishbone was licking up the last bits of dog food from his bowl when he heard Joe's step outside the main cabin door. A moment later, he and David appeared wearing jeans and T-shirts. They smelled of fresh lake water.

"Hi, Joe. Hi, David," Wishbone said. "I'm finishing my breakfast in time to get some of yours. This is the big day! Super Sleuth needs to fuel up."

Ally and her mom were already there, making scrambled eggs, bacon, and toast. Luke was talking on the phone.

"Hi, everyone. That smells great," David said. He got out plates and silverware and began setting the table.

Wishbone watched as Joe walked over to the fireplace. He picked up the brush and dust pan. He looked as if he were about to sweep out the ashes. But instead he stood there, gazing at the cold hearth. He seemed to sink deeper and deeper into thought.

"Joe, you remind me of Tom Sawyer again." Wishbone trotted over and sat at his feet. "He used to think that way. Huck Finn called it 'that brown study.' Then Tom would snap out of it and have everything figured out."

The terrier looked up as Luke hung up the phone.

"I just called the sheriff's office. He's out of town this morning. He'll be back for the auction," Luke said.

"Will there be time to talk to him about the Castles?" David asked.

"Maybe we can have a word with him before the bidding begins," Tina suggested.

Ally carried the steaming eggs and bacon to the table. Luke brought the milk and a pot of coffee. Everyone sat down, except Joe.

"Yo, Talbot," David said. "Chow's on."

Joe looked up, but he didn't seem to see them. "Just a minute," he murmured. "I need to think."

"We'd better start," Tina said. "The food will get—"

Joe dropped the brush and dust pan with a loud clatter. He spun around. He looked as though he might explode with excitement. *"Now* I've got it! Someone give me a hammer—quick!"

"I knew this would happen!" Wishbone said. "Go, Joe!"

Luke looked confused. But he stood up and handed Joe a hammer from the tool drawer. Joe grabbed it and dashed toward the bedroom.

Wishbone followed on his heels. "I know you're onto something big, Joe."

The rest of the group hurried into the bedroom right behind them.

"What are you—" Luke began.

Wishbone danced from paw to paw as Joe tossed the window seat cushion to the floor. He used the hammer to pry the seat away from the wall. The wood boards creaked and groaned as he pulled them back. As soon as the space was large enough, Joe plunged one arm inside. He began feeling around, his eyebrows knit with eagerness and worry.

Everyone else stared at Joe without speaking. No one even seemed to breathe. Wishbone, too, stood still, watching . . .

"Yes!" Joe shouted.

He yanked out his grimy arm and held it high over his head. In his hand was a flat, round object. It was covered with dust. But Wishbone could make out the gleam of gold.

"It's the watch!" Joe shouted. "The Talbot family watch!"

Chapter Sixteen

Wishbone wagged his tail wildly. He barked as everyone rushed up to Joe. David pounded him on the back. Luke shook his free hand. Tina hugged him, and then Ally flung her arms around his shoulders.

"I can't believe it!"

"How did you do it?"

"It's amazing! Astounding!"

"After all these years!"

Joe was grinning from ear to ear. He handed the watch carefully to Luke.

At first, Luke simply stared at it. Then he gently blew off the loose dust. With the tail of his flannel shirt, he wiped the cover. He worked slowly, gently. When he was finished, he opened his hands so everyone could see the result.

Wishbone rose up on his hind legs. There it was. A round cover of rich yellow gold. Two large diamonds that sparkled with blue and green flashes of light. Engraved between the diamonds was the large, fancy "T."

Luke opened the cover. The watch face was ivory-colored. It had gold hands and delicate Roman numerals. Luke read the inscription on the inside of the cover out loud.

"'Josiah Howell Talbot. Twelfth Regiment, Union Army.'" He looked at Joe. "You're named for him. So it's very fitting that you recovered his watch." He paused and added, "Your dad would be mighty impressed. Thank you, Joe."

Joe didn't say anything, but Wishbone knew what he was thinking.

"It's as though you and your dad looked for the watch together," Wishbone said. He rubbed his muzzle against Joe's leg. "But you're the one who found it."

"Aren't you going to tell us how you figured it out?" David asked.

"I'm so surprised, I've got to sit down," Tina said.

She sank down on the desk chair. Luke, David, and Ally sat on the edge of the bed. Wishbone sat back on his haunches and gazed up at his best buddy. "Super Sleuth is all ears."

"Well," Joe said, "I figured it out this way. Tina dropped the watch through the torn screen. But no one found it. So it didn't land on the window seat. There was only one other place where it could land. That was between the window seat and the wall."

"But we looked there," Luke said. "Just the way you did."

Joe smiled. "I know. I read about it in my dad's journal. But you looked there *before* Tina returned the watch."

After a moment's pause, Luke thumped one hand against his forehead. "Of course! We did our search late in the afternoon."

"And I returned the watch hours later," Tina added. "At one-thirty in the morning."

Wishbone sighed. "Ah, the work of a fine detective is elegantly simple. And so very brilliant."

"I also got an idea from Mark Twain's *Tom Sawyer, Detective*," Joe said. "The two missing diamonds in that story weren't really missing. They were right there all the time. Hidden in the heels of Jubiter Dunlap's boots."

Tina eyes lit up. "That's a terrific book. I bought a copy for Ally a while ago. She loved it, too."

"Actually, I have your old copy," Joe said to Tina.

Tina looked amazed. "You do?"

"I found it in our attic last winter. Along with my dad's journal," Joe told her.

"Cool," Ally said. "Can I see my mom's copy some time?"

"If you want, I'll give it back to you," Joe said. "I brought it here with me."

Luke whistled under his breath. "Life sure is full of strange and wonderful connections." He stood up and clapped his hands together. "I need some food to anchor all the excitement. And we've got to plan our strategy for the auction."

As they walked back to the breakfast table, Wishbone looked up at Joe. "You have a nice flair for drama, buddy. You called for that hammer just like Tom Sawyer in the big court-room scene. He called for a screwdriver. Then he took apart Jubiter's boot heel and revealed the diamonds."

Over breakfast, Luke and Tina discussed who else might be bidding at the auction. They decided on the highest bid they could make.

"We should talk to Mac before the auction begins," Luke said. "Maybe we can go over to the McKenzie camp after breakfast."

"I was thinking the same thing," Tina said. "I want to let Mac know I'm here. And we should tell him we're bidding together."

"Shouldn't we let the McKenzies know about the fire?" Joe asked. "And that we're going to talk to the sheriff about the Castles?"

"Definitely," Luke said. "I want to tell Mac about the watch, too. I'll call right now to see if we can go over there."

A few minutes later, Joe watched Wishbone trot ahead of him through the woods. David, Luke, and the Joplins followed single-file behind them. The narrow path wound past the former Tucker camp. The sun was high. It dotted the ground with patches of light. Joe glanced at his watch.

Eleven-thirty! Only two and a half hours until the auction! He took a deep breath to calm the jittery feeling in his stomach. *What if we can't outbid the Castles?*

The path ended in a clearing in front of the MacKenzie house. The comfortable-looking place was built in log-cabin style. Pat's shiny motorcycle stood in the shade next to the MacKenzie's car.

Mac waved from the porch. "You've caught us on laundry day," he said. "We're in the middle of getting everything together. So excuse the disorder."

He ushered them into the cabin right away. Linda MacKenzie was making a pot of coffee. Pat was carrying a pile of laundry into the room. He tossed it onto a footstool and said hello.

"Thanks so much for finding the motorcycle," Linda said, turning to Joe and David. "I don't know how you managed it. But we're all really grateful."

"Yeah, thanks a lot. It's great to have it back," Pat added.

Luke looked at Tina and raised his eyebrows. He seemed to saying, "It's your turn now."

Tina took a deep breath. "Mac . . . I'm Tina Tucker," she said.

Joe wasn't surprised to see the puzzled look on Mac's face. It was as if he didn't understand what she had said. He stared at Tina, and a smile slowly spread across his face.

"Tina? Tina Tucker! It's great to see you again! Really great!"

Tina laughed and gave Mac a hug. She introduced Ally and shook hands with Linda and Pat.

"I've heard lots about you," Linda said. "We even have some pictures of you in an old family album."

For Joe, the next twenty minutes vanished in a stream of intense talk: Luke and Tina's joint bid, the fire in the woodshed, the yellow jacket, the Castles, the sheriff. Joe was so busy listening that he was barely aware of Wishbone prowling around the room, sniffing.

"Something else pretty incredible happened this morning," Luke finally said. "We found the Talbot family heirloom watch."

"What!" Mac looked hard at Luke.

"It's a pretty wild story," Tina said. "And it's my fault the whole thing ever happened."

Joe noticed that Mac didn't say a word while they told him the story.

"Mac, I hope you'll forgive me for ever suspecting you," Luke said. "It was years ago, but it was wrong and unfair."

Mac remained silent. He seemed to be absorbing it all. At last, he said, "I guess Tina's return to the lake can be a new start all around."

"I agree," Luke said. He stood up and stuffed his hands into the pockets of his faded cut-off jeans. "Well, we've landed a lot of news on you folks this morning. But here's one last thing. On the way here, Tina and I were talking more about our bid. We'd be happy to have you MacKenzies join us. I mean, if the idea appeals to you."

Mac looked at Linda, then at Pat. They all seemed unsure. Joe noticed that Pat was actually scowling.

"We've talked so long about having a larger camp," Mac said. "And there's so little time before the auction. Maybe we'd better stick with our separate bid."

"I can understand that," Tina said.

Luke nodded. "Me, too. So we'll just see each other at the Tucker camp in about an hour."

Everyone moved to the door. Joe looked around for Wishbone. The dog was sniffing the laundry heaped on the low stool.

"Wishbone, come on." Joe took a step toward the dog. Wishbone glanced at him. In the next instant, the terrier lunged at the laundry, barking. It all toppled to the floor.

"Wishbone!" Joe said sharply. He dropped onto one knee and began gathering up the laundry. Wishbone had grabbed a faded denim shirt with his teeth. "Come on, boy. Drop it," Joe said.

He gently tugged at it, but Wishbone wouldn't let go. "I don't know what's gotten into him. He's never done this before."

Joe yanked on the shirt again. This time, Wishbone let go. Joe stuffed it into the laundry pile and picked Wishbone up.

"Sorry about that," he said to the MacKenzies.

"No problem," Mac said. "It's all going into the washing machine."

Wishbone barked again. He seemed agitated. Joe headed for the door. "What's going on, boy?"

Two hours later, Wishbone walked nervously around the clearing at the Tucker camp. This is it! he thought.

The peaceful place was completely transformed. About seventy people were crowded into the clearing around the cabin. The bank official and auctioneer stood on the front porch. They had opened the cabin so bidders could inspect it. People were wandering in and out of the building. More and more arrived.

Wishbone pricked up his ears. A nonstop buzz of conversation filled the air.

"Look at all these people," Joe said as Wishbone stopped in front of him. Joe picked up the terrier. "It looks like whole families have come to watch. I wonder who's going to bid?"

Wishbone scanned the crowd with his alert eyes. He thought he could spot the people who had to come to bid. They stood alone or in pairs. They looked serious and didn't talk a lot. They kept checking their watches. Wishbone noticed Ethan and Annette Castle among them. They stood toward the back of the crowd. They were observing the scene just the way Joe was. Now and then, they whispered something to each other.

Wishbone turned his head and saw David tap Joe on the shoulder. "One forty-five," David said, pointing to his wristwatch. "Time's running out. And there's no sign of the sheriff."

Joe looked around anxiously.

"We've got to confront the Castles before the auction," David went on. "If they confess to wrecking Luke's canoe and setting fire to the woodshed, the sheriff might ban them from bidding and—"

The sound of a car door slamming made Wishbone's head turn again. The sheriff's van had stopped near the back of the cabin. He had already jumped out.

Wishbone wagged his tail. "Okay, folks. It's showtime!"

In a flash, Joe, David, Luke, Ally, Tina, and the MacKenzies surrounded Sheriff Eastwood. As they all spoke, Wishbone saw the sheriff's expression grow more and more serious.

Sheriff Eastwood stepped away from Joe's group after a few minutes. Wishbone saw him walk over to Annette and Ethan Castle, who were standing near the back door. Then he motioned for the Castles, as well as Joe's entire group, to follow him into the cabin.

Inside, the sheriff took off his hat and raised his voice. "Folks," the sheriff said with authority. "I'm going to ask you all to exit this building now. The auction will be starting in just a few minutes. You can stand anywhere in the clearing around the building."

As everyone else filed out, the sheriff motioned for Joe's group and the Castles to gather on one side. Joe put Wishbone down. When the last visitor had departed, the sheriff firmly closed and latched the back door. Then he cleared his throat.

Joe's heart pounded as the group formed a loose circle. He positioned himself next to the sheriff. From that spot, he could see everyone else. Wishbone sat at his feet. Sheriff Eastwood cleared his throat.

"Look, friends, I've known most of you for years. And I know you as fine people. But I have a situation on my hands. And I want to deal with it before the auction begins. So excuse me if I'm brief and blunt."

Wishbone waited expectantly until the sheriff continued. "You all know about Luke's vandalized canoe and Pat's stolen motorcycle. Late last night, someone set Luke's woodshed on fire. Now here's the other information I've got. Joe and David found the Castles' key ring . . ."

As the sheriff spoke, Wishbone saw Ethan and Annette glare at Joe and David. Wishbone was proud of the way his boy kept cool and calm. Joe breathed slowly and put his hands into his jeans pockets.

All of a sudden, a puzzled frown appeared on Joe's face. He pulled something from his pocket. A scrap of cloth. Wishbone recognized it at once.

The sheriff's voice went on. "Joe saw someone in a yellow hooded jacket for a second time . . ."

Joe didn't appear to hear. Wishbone could tell he was searching for links, straining to fit pieces of the puzzle together. Joe's eyes shifted. He stared at a spot directly across from him. Mac MacKenzie, Linda, and Pat stood there. As

Joe watched them, Wishbone saw his fingers close around the scrap of cloth. Suddenly Joe clenched his fist hard.

"Yes!" Wishbone said. "He's got it!"

"Joe? Joe!"

Joe's head snapped up as the sheriff spoke to him.

"Joe, we need you to describe exactly what you saw in the woods last night. Did you—"

"For crying out loud!" Ethan Castle interrupted. "The kid isn't even paying attention! But he's going around making accusations and coming up with wild stories. I don't care if someone was wearing a yellow jacket in the Talbot woods. That doesn't mean—"

"What about the key ring?" Mac asked.

"I don't care about that either!" Ethan was almost shouting.

"Okay, everyone calm down," said Sheriff Eastwood.

"Here's the bottom line," Annette Castle said. She kept her voice low, but it was tense. "Neither Ethan nor I destroyed a canoe. We didn't steal a motorcycle. And we didn't set a woodshed on fire."

"That's true."

It was Joe who spoke. Every pair of eyes immediately turned in his direction.

"Take it away, Joe!" Wishbone said. "Show 'em what Super Sleuth has taught you."

"Joe, what are you saying?" Sheriff Eastwood asked.

Joe spoke quietly but without hesitation.

"I'm saying that the Castles had nothing to do with those crimes."

Joe looked straight across the circle.

"The guilty person is Pat MacKenzie."

Chapter Seventeen

Joe looked around at the circle of stunned faces.

"What!" Mac's large green eyes flashed angrily at Joe.

"That couldn't be true!" Linda MacKenzie exclaimed.

She turned to Pat. So did everyone else. Pat stood perfectly still. Then he rubbed his right foot against the back of his left ankle.

Joe pointed to Pat's foot. "There! He just did it again."

"Joe," the sheriff said. There was a touch of impatience in his voice. "I don't know what you're talking about. You've made a serious accusation. So start at the beginning and explain it. And I want everyone else to be quiet until Joe finishes."

Joe nodded and turned to the sheriff.

"Here's what happened," he said. "Pat

knew that Luke always left his canoe at the little dock. On Tuesday, Pat was in Woodwich when Luke met David and me at the bus stop. That's when Pat destroyed the canoe. He left the key ring near the dock to make the Castles look guilty. It was easy for him to take the key ring from the Castles' house because he works there."

"You can't prove any of that," Pat muttered.

One angry look from the sheriff silenced him.

Joe continued. "Pat took the yellow hooded jacket from the Castles' mudroom at least twice. David and I saw him wearing it late Tuesday night in the woods near the Talbot cabin. And I saw him wearing it last night during the fire. That's when I noticed him rub his right foot against his left ankle. Only I didn't know it was Pat then. But since we've been standing here, he's done it twice. And the second time, you all saw it."

The sheriff shook his head slightly. "Joe, this is still guesswork. Rubbing one foot against another is a nervous gesture. There might be other people who do that. You need proof. Solid proof."

"Exactly," Linda said.

Wishbone nudged Joe's leg with his muzzle. "Tell 'em, Joe!"

"Well, here's my proof," Joe said.

He held out his hand. On the open palm lay the scrap of cloth.

The sheriff peered at it. "A torn bit of denim?"

Across the room, Pat started to rub his foot against his ankle. He quickly stopped himself.

"I found this scrap of cloth in the woods behind Gerry Rich's house," Joe explained. "It was caught on some thorns close to where we found the motorcycle. Then just an hour ago, Wishbone knocked over a pile of laundry in the MacKenzie cabin. He got hold of a shirt with a hole in one sleeve. This scrap of cloth matches the shirt exactly."

"Uh, folks . . . " Wishbone looked around the cabin. "I didn't knock over that laundry pile by accident. I recognized Pat's scent at the MacKenzie place. It matched the scent I tracked through the woods to the motorcycle. The shirt smelled like Pat, too. Hey, is anybody listening?"

Mac was looking at his son, but Pat cast his eyes down. "You're saying Pat hid his own motorcycle in the woods and then *pretended* it was stolen?" Mac asked Joe.

Joe nodded. "Pat told the Castles that he couldn't get to the lumber yard on Wednesday afternoon. So the Castles had to go to Woodwich themselves to pick up the lumber. That put them in town when the motorcycle disappeared. The key ring, the yellow jacket, the motorcycle—they all made the Castles look guilty."

Wishbone saw that Joe had convinced the others. Ethan and Annette Castle looked shocked. Linda MacKenzie turned to Pat with tears in her eyes. Mac put his arm around her shoulders. David caught Joe's eye and nodded slightly. Everyone else looked sad.

"Well, Pat?" the sheriff asked. He kept his face neutral, but his voice sounded stern.

Pat looked up at the sheriff. But his eyes quickly dropped down again. "It's true," he said in a low voice.

Sheriff Eastwood sighed. "I suppose you set up the Castles so they wouldn't be allowed to bid. Without them, you thought your parents had a better chance of getting this camp. Right?"

"Pat wants his own place to live in," Mac answered. "Linda and I promised him this cabin if we bought the camp. It seemed like a good idea." He shook his head. "But it wasn't. It was too much of a temptation for him."

The sheriff glanced at his watch. "The rest of this sad business involves the MacKenzies, Luke, and me. Luke's the one whose property was damaged. I want the five of us to meet right after the auction. At the MacKenzie camp? Okay?"

Mac whispered something to Linda. She nodded.

"We'll wait for you at our place," Linda said. "Mac and I don't feel like bidding now."

As the MacKenzies walked out the door, Joe watched them with an unhappy expression in his eyes. Wishbone licked Joe's hand.

"You did the right thing by finding out the truth, Joe. Super Sleuth is proud."

Joe squeezed into the crowd in front of the Tucker cabin. He was glad to have Wishbone at his side.

As David, Luke, and the Joplins gathered next to him, David whispered to Joe, "Way to go! You figured out the whole thing at once."

"I guess so," Joe said in a low voice. "But it wasn't like Tom Sawyer's courtroom scene. Everyone was happy when he proved his uncle was innocent. It was like a celebration. It's the opposite today. I'm really sad for Mac and Linda."

David nodded. Joe could tell he felt the same way.

"Okay, team," Luke said in a low voice. He glanced up at the porch. Sheriff Eastwood stood there with the auctioneer and the bank official.

"We've got about a minute to talk. We're all pretty upset about Pat. But right now we've got to focus on saving Lost Lake. Remember we're saving it for everyone—including our friends and neighbors."

Everyone nodded.

"Tina and I decided that I'll do the actual bidding," Luke went on. "I'm familiar with the crowd here. You all know how high we can bid with the money we've got. But there's one other possibility . . ."

Luke looked straight at Joe. "We could add in the value of the Talbot watch. But I won't do that unless Joe is convinced we should sell it. The watch should belong to him someday. It's an important part of the family history."

Joe opened his mouth to speak, but Luke interrupted him.

"Think about it while the bidding starts. I want you to be absolutely sure."

"I'm sure already," Joe said. "I knew we might need the watch for our bid. That's why I tried so hard to find it. I think my dad would agree that we should use it."

Luke gave Joe's shoulder a quick squeeze. "Then let's—"

Thwack!

The auctioneer banged his gavel on the porch railing just once. The crowd fell silent. Everyone's attention was focused on him. He was a tall man with slicked-back, gray hair. He wore a white shirt, black sports jacket, and blue tie. The sheriff and bank official stood several feet behind him.

"Property number eighty-four of the Woodwich Bank and Trust Company. Located on Moose Cove, Lost Lake." The auctioneer didn't speak loudly. Yet his deep voice carried easily over the crowd. He wasted no time. "Bidding will start at thirty thousand dollars. Do I hear thirty?"

"Thirty," Annette Castle called out.

Joe's heart began beating faster. *Here we go.*

The auctioneer kept his eyes on the crowd. "Do I hear thirty-five?"

"Forty," a man's voice called out from the back.

Every head turned to look at him. He was tall, Joe saw, and wore sunglasses.

"Fifty," Luke called out.

"Fifty," the auctioneer said. "Do I hear sixty?"

"Sixty," a woman in a plaid bandana called out.

"Seventy." It was Annette Castle again.

"Do I hear eighty?" the auctioneer asked.

"Eighty," Luke called out.

"Ninety," came the bid from the man in sunglasses.

Annette Castle raised her hand. "One hundred."

"One hundred five," Luke called out.

Joe knew that Luke was trying to slow down the bidding. He wanted a little more time to react to the other bidders. He and Tina were quickly approaching their limit too quickly. Without the watch, they had to stop at one hundred fifty thousand dollars.

"How much will the watch add?" Joe asked in a whisper.

Luke didn't take his eyes off the auctioneer. "Twenty thousand. Maximum."

The bidding continued. Joe reached down to touch Wishbone's head. The seconds slipped by. So did thousands of dollars.

"One hundred twenty-five."

"One hundred thirty."

"One hundred thirty-five."

There was a pause. Joe saw the woman in the bandana shake her head. She was dropping out.

"Do I hear one hundred forty?" the auctioneer asked.

"One hundred forty," the man in the sunglasses called out.

"One hundred forty-five," Annette Castle said immediately.

"One hundred fifty," Luke called out.

"Do I hear one hundred fifty-five?" the auctioneer asked.

The man with the sunglasses shook his head.

He's out! Joe thought. *Now it's just the Castles and us.*

"One hundred fifty-five," Annette called out.

Luke glanced at Joe. Joe nodded. It was time to use the value of the watch.

"One hundred sixty," Luke called out.

Joe held his breath. Silently, he urged the Castles, *Drop out! Please drop out!*

"One hundred sixty-five," Annette called. She was glaring at Luke.

Luke kept his eyes on the auctioneer. But Joe could see the tension in his jaw.

"One hundred seventy," Luke called out.

Joe's heart pounded. *Uh, oh, that's our limit, he thought.*

No more bids!

Annette nodded at the auctioneer. "One hundred seventy-five."

Joe felt the blood rush to his head. His cheeks burned. Luke bit his lower lip and looked down at the ground.

"Do I hear one hundred eighty?" the auctioneer asked.

The crowd hushed. Joe's heart sank as the auctioneer said, "Going . . . going . . ."

"One hundred eighty."

It was a new voice. Joe and everyone else turned around to see who it was. At the edge of the crowd, with his arms folded across his chest, stood Mac. His green eyes stared straight ahead.

Annette Castle scowled. "One hundred eighty-five."

"One hundred ninety," Mac said.

He turned slightly, and his eyes met Luke's. He nodded.

"Mac's bidding with us!" Luke said in a low voice.

Hope surged through Joe's body like a bolt of electricity. David, Tina, and Ally all looked as if they could hardly stand the suspense.

Annette whispered something to Ethan Castle. She turned to the auctioneer. "One hundred ninety-five."

"Two hundred," Mac said immediately.

Annette and Ethan turned to look at him. Mac kept his eyes on the auctioneer. He didn't move a muscle.

"Do I hear two hundred five?" the auctioneer asked.

Silence. Slowly the auctioneer raised his gavel.

"Going . . . going . . ."

Joe held his breath.

Thwack!

"Sold!"

The silence around Joe shattered with shouts of joy. Joe heard himself cheering along with his friends. Wishbone was barking. Everyone in their group was hugging everyone else. They were pounded each other on the back. When Mac walked up to them, Luke and Tina had tears in their eyes.

"It's a dream," Tina said as she hugged Mac. "A dream come true."

Chapter Eighteen

It was Monday evening. The late sun seeped into the woods in narrow, slanting rays. They warmed Wishbone's nose as he trotted along-side Joe down the path that led from the Tal-bot's main cabin to their cabin.

Wishbone sniffed the air. "Ah, a soothing blend of pine and maple tonight." He sighed. "I really do like this place. I'm sorry we're leaving tomorrow morning."

When they reached their cabin, Joe swung open the door. "Got it!" he said to David. He held up a small, smooth object. "Luke's penknife.

David was sitting on his bed with the com-puter on his lap. When he saw the knife, a smile spread across his face. "Great," he said. "I'll be ready in a second. I'm finishing up our case files."

Joe sat down next to him and looked at the

computer screen. He read what he saw there out loud.

```
CASE: MISSING TALBOT WATCH.
STATUS: UNSOLVED.
CASE: SABOTAGED CANOE &
AUCTION. STATUS: UNSOLVED.
```

David tapped a few keys. The electronic words blinked and shifted.

Joe grinned as he read the new version. "Case closed. Case closed."

David exited the program and shut off the computer.

"It's pretty amazing how perfectly everything worked out," Joe said. "Except for Pat. But Luke says he'll get help from a counselor. Luke thinks the year of community service will be good for Pat, too."

"And Luke agreed not to press charges against him. Sounds like a fair deal," David said. He paused and added, "I'm really glad Mac won't let Luke sell the Talbot watch."

Wishbone agreed. "That makes two of us!"

He had been present the day before when Mac had stopped by to speak to Luke. Mac wanted his bid to cover the value of the gold watch, so that the watch could stay in the Talbot family.

Glancing at his best buddy, Wishbone saw how very satisfied Joe looked. "Correction. That makes *three* of us!"

David glanced at the wood-paneled wall above the beds. "Let's do it, Talbot," he said.

"You first." Joe handed him the penknife.

David kicked off his shoes and stood on his mattress. With the knife's carving blade, he pointed to the initials already carved into the wall.

"Below Luke's initials or to the side?" he asked.

Joe gazed at the wall for a moment. "To the side."

Pressing the blade into the wood, David began to carve. A few minutes later, he revealed the result.

L.T. D.B.

"How does it look?" David asked.

"Good," Joe said. "It looks like it was meant to be that way."

Joe took the knife and began working on the wall above his own bed. Wishbone stretched out on the bed at his feet. When Joe finished, Wishbone saw new initials carved next to the old ones.

"Pretty neat," David said.

"Pretty incomplete, if you ask me." Wishbone sat up and scratched the wall with one paw. Joe looked down at him.

"You know, I should carve Wishbone's initials, too."

Wishbone wagged his tail. "Joe, you're

always on top of things. With a little help from me, of course."

After a few minutes, Joe showed off his handiwork.

S.T. J.T. WB

"Excellent," Wishbone gazed at the newly carved initials. "Thanks for—"

Thwack! BANG!

Someone had pushed the door open hard. It swung on its hinges and slammed against the table.

"They've hatched! The loons!" Ally Joplin stood in the doorway, out of breath. "Come quick!"

She whirled around and started running back down the shoreline path. Joe closed the pocket knife and tossed it onto the bed. David was already dashing out the door. Wishbone and Joe were right behind him.

"Loon chicks!" Wishbone exclaimed as he ran. "*My* loon chicks. Whoopee-e-e!"

As they approached the spit of land, they all slowed down. Luke and Tina were up ahead, crouched in the brush on the shore. Ally, Joe, David, and Wishbone joined them. Wishbone glanced inside the loon nest. All that remained there were pieces of olive-brown eggshell. He sniffed at the broken pieces, then glanced up at Ally in alarm.

"They're gone!"

"Where?" Joe began.

Ally put a finger to her lips. She pointed to the tip of the spit of land.

There they were. The entire loon family appeared on the tip of the spit of land. The two adult loons swam side by side. Nestled on each one's back was a tiny creature—soft, round, and covered in gray fluff. Wishbone could just make out dark little eyes and bills. The chicks looked comfortable and secure between the folded wings of their parents.

Wishbone's whiskers trembled with excitement. "A new generation swims forth under the proud eye of the knight in shining fur."

He watched as the loons circled around the spit of land. Then they turned and headed for deeper water farther out in the cove.

"When did they hatch?" David asked.

"I'd say about three hours ago," Tina said. "As soon as the chicks dry out, they're ready to leave the nest. They're safer on the water."

"Will they go back to the nest at night?" Joe asked.

Luke shook his head. "Nope, they'll live on the water from now on. But the chicks will stay very close to the adults for a couple of weeks."

Tina stood up and stretched her legs. "I'm going to call the Loon Preservation Society. It'll want to get the birth announcement out right away."

"Birth announcement?" Joe asked. "You're kidding."

"Believe me, this is a *big* deal," Tina said. "The society does a flyer for every chick that's born. It'll post the news all over town."

"I heard they've been worried about this pair," Luke added. "These chicks are the last to hatch, and they're pretty late."

Ally bent down and hugged Wishbone. "But they made it, thanks to Wishbone."

"You know something, Ally," Wishbone said. "I like your attitude toward the furred and feathered."

Ally stood up and looked at Joe and David. "I'm so jazzed about this I can't stand still. Want to race across the cove? I've got enough energy to beat you both."

"You're on," David said.

He and Joe immediately headed for the cabin to change.

"Meet you on the Talbot dock," Joe called over his shoulder. "Five minutes to splash-off!"

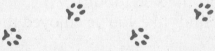

It was almost midnight. Wishbone was stretched out on the Talbot dock, under the starry sky. Luke was playing the guitar. Joe, David, Tina, and Ally sang along with him. They repeated the chorus of an old Beatles tune one last time.

As the final chord died out, Wishbone heard the gentle sound of canoe paddling. A few seconds later, a boat slid up to the dock.

Luke leaned forward and peered into the darkness. "Mac?"

"None other," Mac said. "I heard the singing and couldn't resist it. Sounds like old times."

"You've got to join us," Tina said. "We need your deep voice for harmony."

"Come on. There's just enough room," Luke said.

Everyone squeezed closer together as Mac climbed onto the dock.

"So you're leaving already," Mac said to Joe and David. "I hope you'll be back next summer."

"Definitely!" Joe and David said together.

"I've made them promise to bring Joe's mom next summer. And David's family. And their other best friend, Sam. I gather she's a girl," said Luke.

Joe grinned. "Samantha Kepler. You'd like her a lot," he said to Ally.

"Sounds like you've enjoyed the lake," Mac said.

"It's an awesome place," David replied. "Actually, I was sort of surprised at how much I liked it. It's different from my usual thing . . . simpler, maybe."

Ally laughed. "I used to think my mom was

exaggerating about Lost Lake. But she was right."

"This calls for a old favorite," Luke said. He strummed the guitar and started singing a familiar folk song, "This Land is Your Land." After one verse, everyone joined in. Everyone but Wishbone, though his tail wagged in time to the beat. Bright stars, good friends, fun songs. What's not to like?

They sang the entire song twice. Joe didn't want the evening to end. He knew that none of them did. But finally, they had to say good-night.

When he and David returned to their cabin, Joe saw the camp log lying on his bed.

"Have you written in it yet?" he asked David.

"Yep." David nodded. "Earlier tonight."

"Me, too," Joe said. "But I want to add Wishbone's paw print."

Joe patted some water onto the bottom of Wishbone's right front paw. "The water should get muddy enough to leave a mark."

Joe pressed the dog's paw against a blank page in the log. He held it there for a minute. It left a gray-brown print.

"Excellent pawmanship," Joe said, showing the mark to David.

"A-plus." David pulled his blanket over his shoulders. "Well, good-night."

"'Night." Joe put the open log on the table so the paw print would dry.

The next morning dawned clear and bright. By ten o'clock, Joe, David, and Wishbone were settled in the comfortable bus, starting for home. Sitting next to each other, Joe and Wishbone gazed out their window. The dog pressed his moist nose against the glass as they rolled past the white wood-framed houses. David sat across the aisle, staring out his window.

The bus gathered speed and left the town of Woodwich behind.

Joe rubbed the fur between Wishbone's ears. "Good-bye to Lost Lake," he murmured. "But just for now. We'll be back." A smile turned up the corners of his mouth. "It's been quite a week, hasn't it, Wishbone?"

Joe took his dad's journal and a pen out of the backpack stored under his seat. He opened the notebook to the last page, which was only half-filled. Wishbone turned around to see what his friend was doing just as Joe began to write on the blank part of the page.

July 12. My first visit to Lost Lake has ended. I found the missing Talbot watch—and a missing part of Steve Talbot's life. At least it was missing for me. Now it feels like I've shared his past and it'll be part of my future. But none of it would have happened without this journal. So thanks, Dad, from your son, Joe.

About Joanne Barkan

The English writer John Fowles once said that every person has his or her own paradise on earth. He meant that we all can find a real place that feels wonderfully special and where we are deeply happy. For Joanne Barkan, that place is Squam Lake in central New Hampshire.

Almost every summer for the last twenty years, she has visited friends who have a "camp" on this beautiful lake. When she began creating a story for WISHBONE Super Mysteries, she decided that a lake just like Squam would make a great setting. That's how *Riddle of the Lost Lake* was born.

Joanne began to write books for young people while she was working with the Muppets. She's now a full-time writer and the author of more than 110 children's books, including middle-grade fiction, non-fiction, early-reader stories, picture books, and preschool concept books.

Joanne lives in Manhattan with her husband, Jon R. Friedman, who is a painter and sculptor. They love the crowded city with all its skyscrapers, museums, and theaters. They also enjoy the community flower garden in Riverside Park just around the corner from their apartment building. They spend summers on Cape Cod, a long, thin peninsula along the coast of Massachusetts. They've built a house and studio on a sand dune there.

Come aboard with Wishbone for a fascinating undersea adventure coming your way next month in Twenty Thousand Wags Under the Sea. *Here's a sneak preview . . .*

Chapter One

"Ooh! Ooh!" Wishbone pressed his muzzle against the car window. "There's another canoe! On top of the blue van." The white Jack Russell terrier with black and brown spots tapped the window with a paw and wagged his tail. "That's the tenth one. I win the game!"

Joe Talbot, Wishbone's best buddy, sat beside the terrier in the back seat of the rented car. "Number ten!" the boy declared. He tugged his blue baseball cap farther down over his brown hair. "I spotted ten canoes first."

Wishbone tore his eyes from the tropical scenery that rolled past the car window. He gave Joe a friendly lick on the nose and said, "Who saw ten canoes first?"

Wishbone and his friends had flown to Orlando, Florida, the evening before, from their hometown of Oakdale. After spending the night in a motel near the airport, they'd gotten on the road early. They were playing games to pass the time. Joe's mom, Ellen Talbot, was driving. She had suggested counting canoes, because many of the cars on the highway carried them on roof racks.

Joe and Wishbone's good friend Samantha Kepler sat next to Ellen in the front seat. David Barnes was buckled in beside Wishbone and Joe in back. David was Joe and Wishbone's other good friend. All three kids were in the same sixth-grade class at school.

Samantha—"Sam" for short—turned toward the back seat and flashed a sunny smile. "I bet Wishbone saw that last canoe before you did, Joe." She reached through the seats and scratched Wishbone behind his spotted ear. "Didn't you, boy?"

"Ahh." The terrier sighed happily. "I can always count on you to listen to the dog, Sam."

The terrier glanced out the window. "Hey! That tree's got bananas on it!" He scrambled over Joe's lap to get a better look.

"Wishbone seems pretty excited," David commented.

"So am I." Joe shoved back his baseball cap. "AquaLand sounds really cool, Mom."

"It should be fun," Ellen said. "Margot really loves her job there."

"Thanks for inviting us along," added Sam.

"Yeah, thanks," David chimed in.

Wishbone wagged his tail. "The more the merrier!" Wishbone had heard Ellen talk about her college friend Margot. She was a veterinarian at the AquaLand Aquarium. Wishbone was looking forward to meeting her. Any doctor who specialized in caring for animals was A-OK with him!

"We can all thank Margot," Ellen said. "She's the one who suggested we fly down here during spring break." She smiled at David in the rearview mirror. "It should be great. AquaLand is the main attraction. But there's lots else to do. There's a huge national park surrounding the aquarium. St. John's River runs right through it. The brochures Margot sent mention all kinds of hiking and boating activities."

"Cool. Hey! There's the sign," David said.

"'Welcome to Riverside National Park, home of AquaLand,'" Ellen read. She turned the rental car onto a smaller, tree-lined road. "Look at that Spanish moss!" she exclaimed.

"Is that anything like a Spanish omelet?" Wishbone wondered. "After hours on the road, I could use a little snack. Then again, I can always use a snack."

Wishbone gazed at the long, droopy greenery that hung from the oak trees along the road. It looked interesting—but not very appetizing.

Joe leaned across Wishbone to gaze out the window. "Awesome palm trees," he said.

David grinned. "We're definitely not in Oakdale anymore."

"That's for sure," Sam agreed.

"A week of fun in the sun," Ellen added from the front seat. "Just think of all the cold, drizzling rain we left behind. I might even go home with a tan."

Wishbone gazed down at his white fur, spotted with brown and black. "No such luck for the dog. Anyone wearing a full-time fur coat doesn't tan."

They drove under an enormous archway of flowering vines. "Here's the entrance to AquaLand," Ellen announced.

Tropical bushes trimmed in the shapes of dolphins, whales, and fish decorated the lawn. Ellen pulled up alongside a pink and turquoise guardhouse.

The attendant checked their names on the guest roster and gave them a map.

"Thanks." Ellen took the map from the guard, then drove around to the parking lot.

Wishbone was glad when Joe pushed open the door. The terrier bounded out of the car and stretched. "Free again!" The sun shone brightly, warming his fur. Seagulls soared across the brilliant blue sky. His keen ears picked up unusual barks, caws, and squeaks that he couldn't begin to identify.

"Listen to all those critters saying hello. We can't keep them waiting!" Wishbone said.

Ellen and Joe consulted the map the guard had given them. "We go straight past the marine mammal habitats," Joe said.

"Follow the dog!" Wishbone trotted along the path.

"Check out the cool habitat," Sam said. She stopped next to a large pool surrounded by cliff and caves.

"Helllooo?" Wishbone barked out. "Anybody home?"

David read the sign on the guardrail. "Three sea otters live in here," he said. "It says they were rescued from an oil spill."

"Where? Where?" Wishbone rose up on his hind legs for a better look.

He didn't see any water creatures. A teenage girl wearing the park uniform was just stepping out onto one of the cliffs. She reached into a pouch slung across her body and pulled out a handful of fish. As if on cue, three otter heads popped out of the water.

"So there they are. Looks like we got here just in time for breakfast." Wishbone wagged his tail, watching.

Wishbone watched the otters as they munched on the raw fish in their front paws. They held their food on their stomachs and kicked their back legs to keep moving. After they finished their snacks, they flipped over.

Looks like fun, Wishbone thought.

A loud barking sound caught Wishbone's attention. He darted over to the next habitat. "That sounds like a dog!"

Instead of a fellow canine, Wishbone saw a dark brown sea lion. It sat on a rock, barking at a park attendant. The young man held a fish in his hand. When the sea lion sat up and clapped its front flippers together, the attendant dropped the fish into its mouth.

"Good boy," the attendant said to the sea lion. He pulled another fish from his pouch.

"I can do that!" Wishbone sat back on his haunches. He clapped his front paws together and barked. "Tah-dah! Hey! Where's my snack?"

"I think Wishbone wants a reward, too," Sam said, laughing. She patted his head. "Good boy."

"What, no sushi?" Wishbone cocked his head to the side. "Never mind. I'm more of a meat-and-ginger-snaps kind of dog."

"Margot's going to wonder what happened to us," Ellen said. "We should get going."

Wishbone was as eager as his friends to explore every habitat. So many smells and sights called out to him! But he followed Ellen obediently to the coral reef exhibit.

"Ellen!" A woman with dark curly hair strode down the ramp toward them.

"Hello, Margot," Ellen said, giving the woman a hug. "It's so great to see you!" Then she introduced everyone.

"Welcome to AquaLand," Margot said with smile. "Sorry I couldn't meet you out front. Since we're here, why don't we start your tour with the coral reef exhibit?"

"Sounds great!" Ellen agreed.

Wishbone trotted up the ramp behind Margot. At the top, he found himself on a wooden dock that surrounded a large, deep tank. His toenails clicked on the wooden boards. He stopped next to the tank alongside Ellen, Sam, and Joe. While they all gazed down at the brightly colored coral, David strolled along the dock.

"Our exhibit is designed so that visitors can look at the reef from here," Margot said. "Or they can view it from the underwater ride."

"You have a submarine?" David asked, his brown eyes widening.

"Not exactly." Margot smiled. "Come on, I'll show you."

Margot led them to a glass elevator beside the entrance. "We have a glass-walled boat under the platform," she told them. "This elevator will bring us right down to it."

"'Down the Hatch,'" Sam read from the driftwood sign hanging on the elevator door. She shrugged, then stepped into the elevator.

Wishbone followed along with everyone else. "Next stop, coral reef," he said.

Margot pressed a button and the elevator descended. "Coral is an amazing habitat," she said. "It provides shelter and food for all kinds of sea life."

"Kind of like an underwater forest," David commented.

"Exactly," Margot agreed.

They came to a stop. The door opened directly into a boat. Sheets of thick glass formed a large glass room. Cushioned benches lined each side. Just outside, coral branches danced in the gentle waves in the tank.

"Wow. We'll have a great view of the reef in this," Joe said, looking all around.

"It's fantastic," David murmured. "It feels like we're part of the reef."

"That's the idea," Margot said. She slid the boat's glass door shut. "This baby is water-tight and has enough air for a two-hour tour. Of course, we'll only be down here for twenty minutes or so. Everyone grab a seat, and I'll take you for the ride."

Wishbone leapt up onto a bench. He pressed his nose to the glass, but he couldn't smell anything. The others found seats around him, and

Margot got them underway. The boat began cruising slowly around the immense coral reef.

Wishbone watched tiny fish dart in and out of the remarkable coral structures. *It's like a fish city,* he thought. *I feel as if I've entered a very strange and very watery new world.*

One of his ears cocked up. *Why does this feel so familiar?* he wondered. *What does this remind me of?*

Let's see . . . An underwater vessel that allows its passengers to see brand new sights. Of course! This is like riding in the *Nautilus*—the amazing submarine created by Jules Verne for his classic novel *Twenty Thousand Leagues Under the Sea.*

In the 1800s Jules Verne entertained readers with stories of strange worlds and unusual inventions. In *Twenty Thousand Leagues Under the Sea*, he sent his characters on an extraordinary journey around the world—underwater.

Watching the tropical fish from the glass boat, it was easy for Wishbone to imagine he was Pierre Aronnax, the French scientist in Jules Verne's classic underwater adventure. In the story, Pierre discovered there was something very fishy going on!

Chapter Two

Wishbone pictured himself as Pierre, dressed in the suit a distinguished professor would wear in 1867. He saw himself in a hotel room in New York, surrounded by a collection of marine specimens. Pierre was an expert on creatures living in the ocean. He was looking forward to going back to his job at the Museum of Natural History in Paris. But Pierre was going to be taking a very long way home . . .

In 1866, strange and mysterious events took place at sea. Ships from many countries reported seeing an enormous "something" hundreds of feet long. By all reports, it moved with incredible speed, was larger than the biggest whale, and was said to glow with an eerie light. Even I, Pierre Aronnax, a scientist and logical dog, was caught up in the excitement and wonder.

Wild stories appeared in newspapers all over the world. Scientists argued endlessly:

could there really be a monster? Was there something living deep under the waves that we had never seen before?

Early in 1867, the problem of the monster stopped being a matter of science and one of safety. Ships were being sunk. One of them, the *Scotia*, was examined after it limped back to port badly damaged. This created even more questions.

The engineers discovered a perfectly shaped triangular hole in the ship's steel hull! What could have made it? A rock? A floating reef? Or a monster with the power to rip through one of the best ocean liners ever built? The public clamored for authorities to rid the ocean of such a danger.

But how? That could only be determined once the true identity of the monster was discovered. As the author of the book, *Mysteries of the Sea,* I was considered an authority. The moment I and my servant, Conseil, returned from our latest expedition, I was consulted by several newspapers. I confessed I was as puzzled as everyone else. Still, the reporters repeatedly questioned me. Finally I told them the only explanation I could think of—the so-called monster was some kind of giant narwhal.

The narwhal is a large, powerful creature related to the beluga whale. Its nickname is "the unicorn of the sea" because of its long tusk. I imagined this tusk might produce the same kind of hole that had nearly sunk the *Scotia*.

"Conseil," I called. My servant was in the other room of the hotel suite arranging our new specimens. "What do you think of all these rumors of a sea monster?"

I spread the newspaper open with my front paws and eagerly scanned the headlines searching for news of the creature.

Conseil came into the room carrying a jar of sea anemones, part of our new collection. "The ocean is of such depth we may never discover all of its secrets," he replied. "Still, I would be quite surprised if there were a monster, as one might find in a child's fairy tale. I believe as the professor does. That the most likely candidate is a giant narwhal."

My tail wagged. Conseil was a most learned and agreeable sort—even if he did have the odd habit of addressing me in the third person. He was the most formal person I have ever known. I've grown used to his ways. He has been with me now for ten years.

"Yes, it must be a narwhal," I declared. "But it must be the biggest narwhal ever to swim in the ocean."

"Is the professor aware that the creature has been sighted again?" Conseil put down the jar and began to take notes on its contents.

I nodded and ran my paw along the lines in

the newspaper article. "An expedition to catch the beast has been arranged. The ship is leaving today!" I exclaimed.

"As we head for Paris, Commander Farragut will be starting on an ocean voyage." Conseil went into the other room to catalogue the next item.

I leapt down from the table to answer a knock at the door. I opened it and a hotel clerk handed me a message:

To Professor Aronnax:
I hope you will agree to join our expedition.
Commander Farragut has a cabin at your
disposal aboard the *Abraham Lincoln.*
Sincerely,
J. B. Hobson,
Secretary of the Navy

My tail thumped wildly back and forth. Join the expedition? Of course I would join the expedition! I leapt into the air and twirled. I had just landed on all four paws when Conseil re-entered the room.

"Has the professor received good news?" he asked.

"Conseil," I ordered as certainly as I could. "Make our preparation. We leave in two hours."

"As you please, sir," he replied.

"And make arrangements to forward the collection to France."

"We are not returning with it, to Paris?" Conseil asked.

"We are returning," I responded. "But, er, ah, well, we will be making a detour."

"Will the detour please you, sir?"

What a fine lad! Always thinking of me. Conseil was as loyal as man's best friend, the noble canine. "Yes," I replied enthusiastically. "It will please me greatly! We just won't be taking a very direct route. We will be traveling aboard the . . . the . . . the *Abraham Lincoln.*"

I knew Conseil would recognize the significance of the ship.

"As you think proper," Conseil said. Calm, as always.

My whiskers quivered. I could no longer contain my excitement. "We're going after the monster!" I exclaimed. "I know the way may be dangerous, but how could I, the author of *Mysteries of the Sea,* I, of all people! How could I turn down such a request?" I paced the room, my nails clicking on the floor. "A glorious mission, but a treacherous one. Who knows where the animal shall lead us? And such a creature! It has the power to break a ship as easily as crack open a nut. But go we must!"

"Then go we shall. I will arrange for a cab," Conseil said. He picked up the house phone and gave instructions.

I glanced around the room. Somehow, while I was talking about our mission, Conseil had managed to pack. The lad was a wonder. In moments we were heading for the docks.

I leapt out of the cab before it came to a complete stop. Who could wait? I was eager to start the voyage! I bounded up the deck and trotted onto the ship.

"Ahh! Sea air!" My whiskers trembled as I lifted my muzzle into the crisp wind. I glanced back at the pier and saw Conseil taking care of the luggage.

Sailors bustled about me, making preparations. I asked a sturdy fellow to direct me to the captain. But it was unnecessary.

"Welcome aboard, Professor." A handsome man in his forties approached me. His manner and his uniform told me he was Commander Farragut.

"It is an honor to join you." I held up my paw, and he grasped it in a warm shake.

"Shall I show you the ship?" he offered.

"Excellent!" I trotted along beside him, eager to explore every corner of my new home. The *Abraham Lincoln* was a frigate, or war ship, of great speed. Three masts towered above us. Sailors scurried around in the rigging, getting ready. Commander Farragut pointed out how well-armed the frigate was for this dangerous mission.

After a tour of the engine room, the captain left me at my cabin. Conseil was already there, finding places for everything, even in those cramped quarters.

"Let us take a last look at solid ground," I suggested to Conseil. "There is no way to guess how long it will be before we return to land."

"As the professor wishes," Conseil said.

We went above deck. Commander Farragut had already given the orders to release the ropes from the moorings. Had we arrived at the docks just a few minutes later, the ship would have sailed without us.

The boat lurched slightly, and I planted my four paws more firmly. We were officially underway.

The piers were crowded with spectators. My fur tingled with pride as I listened to the cheers and watched the thousands of handkerchiefs waving at us. The dock grew smaller and smaller as the *Abraham Lincoln* pulled away, heading for the open sea.

I sat back on my haunches and took in a deep breath of the salty sea air. The adventure had begun!

Commander Farragut had no doubt that he would find the sea monster. He had sworn to rid the seas of it, and he was a man of his word.

All of his officers agreed with him. Each sailor enthusiastically did his share. To add to their eagerness, Commander Farragut offered a reward of two thousand dollars to the first man to spot the monster. Sailors could be found at all hours—day and night—up in the rigging or prowling the decks, their eyes straining to see into the ocean. I confess, it was how I spent most of my time, as well.

In addition to the loyal and courageous crew, Commander Farragut had the best ship ever built for the job. Even more important, the commander had a secret weapon. That secret weapon was Ned Land.

Ned Land was a master harpoonist. He had a keen eye and a powerful arm. The stocky blond fellow came from a long line of Canadian whalers. His stories of whale-hunting were vastly entertaining. Conseil, Ned, and I spent many hours debating the nature of the monster we were chasing. To my shock, Ned didn't believe the creature existed!

"Ned," I exclaimed. "Why do you doubt the possibility of a giant narwhal?"

"You have seen many great sea mammals," Conseil pointed out. I knew that he would be on my side. "Why can't this one exist?"

"That's just it, fellas," Ned explained. "I've hunted and harpooned hundreds, maybe thousands of whales. The biggest anyone has ever seen. Not one of them could have cracked the hull of the *Scotia*."

"But—" I tried to argue, but Ned waved a hand and stopped me.

"A wooden hull, maybe," Ned continued. "But the hull of the *Scotia* was solid steel. There is no way to convince me any ocean creature could pierce it."

Conseil and I exchanged a look. "All right, Ned." I was determined to make the stubborn man see my point. "Think about this. Say this creature lives far deeper in the ocean than any creature we know. Then it would have to be stronger than anything we can imagine."

"Oh, Professor?" Ned raised a quizzical eyebrow. "Why is that?"

"In order to withstand the pressure from all that ocean water," I explained. "Think about it. If you were to find yourself miles under the ocean you'd be flattened like a pancake. Your body isn't built for it. So any mammal living at such a depth must be built to resist thousands of pounds of pressure!"

"Such a creature would have to be made of thick iron plates!" Ned exclaimed.

"Exactly!" I smiled with satisfaction. "Think of what destruction such a powerfully built animal could cause."

Ned frowned. "Perhaps," he said. "But that

doesn't mean I believe such a creature exists!"
He stalked away, shaking his head.

"It seems the Canadian has not been
convinced," Conseil said.

"Not yet . . ." I murmured.

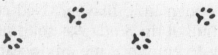

Weeks passed, then months, without a sign
of the monster. The crew made feeble jokes that
the creature knew we were searching for it, so it
went into hiding. But the strain was beginning
to show. Perhaps Ned had been right—there
was no monster

Late one night, Conseil and I strolled along
the deck.

"I'm sorry to have dragged you on this
useless mission," I told him.

"I only regret losing time to classify the
Professor's new specimens," Conseil said.

Suddenly my whiskers quivered. What is
that odd scent? I thought. It's almost electrical.
But how can that be? There is no electricity out
here in the open sea!

I whipped my head around, searching for
the source of the strange smell. I found nothing.

Before I could ask Conseil about it, Ned
Land's voice rang out.

"There it is!" Ned shouted from the crow's
nest. "Our quarry! The beast—straight ahead!"

My heart leapt in my furred chest. Sailors rushed around me as Commander Farragut bellowed orders. Conseil and I raced to the side of the ship. I placed my front paws on the railing. I peered into the night. And gasped.

An enormous object, over two hundred feet long, was visible in the dark water. Visible because it glowed! That was the source of the electrical smell, I realized. It came from the creature.

Is it charged with electricity like an electric eel? I wondered. *What a scientific discovery!*

"It's getting away!" Ned shouted.

"Not under my command," Commander Farragut declared. "Full steam ahead!"

My tail wagged. I was thrilled that soon I would examine this monster up close.

But then—the creature vanished! The glow blinked into darkness. It was as if a light switch had been turned off. The huge black shape sank into the depths of the ocean.

Cries went up from the crew. "Where is it?" "Where did it go?" "What happened?"

Ned's voice rang out above the others. "It's moved to starboard!" he shouted.

"What manner of creature are we facing?" Commander Farragut wondered. "To be able to move so quickly . . ."

Ned clambered down from the crow's nest. He dashed over to the captain. "Sir, if you bring me in close enough, I can sink a harpoon into the creature."

Commander Farragut nodded. "Go to your post. I will give the orders."

"It's getting away!" a sailor yelled.

Ned raced to grab a harpoon. He gripped a rope in one hand and clutched his harpoon in the other.

I trotted to the other side of the ship with Conseil alongside me. The monster had reappeared. Once again it glowed with an eerie green light. It was racing away from us.

The *Abraham Lincoln* gave chase.

"Fire!" Commander Farragut ordered. I heard a low rumble, then the blasting sound of cannon fire. A hit!

The creature came to a stop. Had we injured it? I peered down below at Ned. He was leaning over the water. He raised his harpoon.

"It's heading straight toward us!" I realized.

The dark shape had changed direction. It now sped straight toward the *Abraham Lincoln*. It had no fear at all!

Ned hurled the harpoon. It glanced off the beast's side and vanished into the sea.

I heard a deafening crash. The monster has rammed us! I thought.

In the next instant I was swept overboard—into the dark and churning ocean.

Chapter Three

I paddled furiously with all four paws. I pushed my muzzle through the surface of the water. "Help!" I cried. "Over here!"

Had anyone seen me go overboard? Then another thought hit me, Is the ship still in one piece?

I peered into the darkness. I caught a glimpse of the *Abraham Lincoln* floating at a strange angle. It must be damaged, I realized. Worse, it was already some distance away—and heading away from me. I shouted again. "Help!"

I strained to keep my muzzle above water. But my soaked fur and clothes weighed me down. I couldn't fight against the pull. Down I went. Down . . . Down . . .

All at once a strong hand grabbed my collar. My four legs dangled uselessly as I was pulled back up to the surface. In moments, I was taking in deep gasps of air.

"If Master would be so good as to lean on my shoulder, Master would swim more easily," a calm voice said in my ear.

"Conseil!" I exclaimed. I lay a paw on his shoulder and treaded water with my other three legs.

"Yes, sir. Awaiting my master's instructions."

"Did the impact of the crash throw you overboard too?" I kicked my hind legs to stay afloat.

"No," the lad replied. "But since I am in my master's service, I followed my master."

I was so stunned by Conseil's devotion I nearly went under again. "And the frigate?" I sputtered, spitting salt water out of my mouth.

"I am afraid it was badly damaged. I fear no one on board noticed our disappearance."

"Then we are lost!" I cried.

"Perhaps," Conseil replied. He showed an amazing ability to stay calm! "However, we can certainly survive several more hours. One can accomplish a lot in that time."

"You're right!" I agreed. "Once they discover we are missing, they may come looking for us." I felt a glimmer of hope surge beneath my fur.

Conseil insisted I keep a paw on his shoulder. I leaned heavily against him as we slowly dogpaddled toward the frigate. Every so often, one of us would shout for help, hoping our weak voices would carry. I was growing more and more tired. I knew Conseil was struggling with my added weight. I couldn't let him continue to sacrifice himself for me.

"You must let me go, Conseil," I panted. "I am slowing you down."

"Leave my master?" he gasped. "Never! I would drown first."

My tail wagged feebly. I had no strength to declare my gratitude. In truth, I had no strength left at all. I heard Conseil shouting weakly for help as the world went dark around me.

When I returned to consciousness, I thought I was either dead or dreaming! I lay on something solid, and two friendly faces gazed down at me. Conseil and . . . Ned Land!

"Ned!" I leapt to my paws and shook out my fur, spraying them both with water. "Were you thrown overboard too?"

"I was indeed, Professor," Ned replied. "I was luckier than you two. I landed near this floating island."

"Island?" My paws were covered by ocean water, but they were definitely planted on solid ground.

"Or, more correctly," Ned continued. "On your giant narwhal."

"What?" I stared at Ned. "What do you mean?"

Ned chuckled. "I discovered why my harpoon didn't pierce the beast. Because the creature is made of steel!"

Conseil knelt down and knocked on the surface of our refuge. I heard a clanging sound.

I reached in all directions with my paws. Smooth. Hard . . .

Whoa! Slippery!

I scrambled back upright. No doubt about it. This monster was made of metal.

"I knew there had to be an explanation,"Ned added. "I've never missed my mark yet. Only a creature made of iron plates could best Ned Land!"

My tail wagged with excitement. "Do you know what this means?"

Conseil nodded. "We have discovered a submersible vessel," he said. "And a vessel means a crew."

"Which means we're saved!" I finished.

Ned crossed his arms over his thick chest. "Only if the crew realizes we're here before they decide to take this thing for a dive."

My tail stopped in mid-wag. Ned was right. "We'll have to make our presence known," I declared. "Quickly."

Ned and Conseil knelt down and pounded on the submarine. I howled, barked, and yelped as loudly as I could. The whole time, my mind reeled. Who manned this strange boat? Why had it been built? How did it work? Did the crew know that outsiders thought they were a sea monster?

My speculations were brought to an abrupt end by a loud clanking noise.

"I believe we have been discovered," Conseil commented.

He was right. A hatch popped open in front of us. Several men swarmed out of it. They grabbed Conseil and a protesting Ned and dragged them below.

"I have no plans to struggle—oomph!" My words were cut off as one of the men roughly clutched my collar. I slipped on a narrow ladder and landed below on all four paws.

The hatch overhead slid shut, plunging us into total darkness. I heard Ned swearing, and then a door open. I was shoved into what I imagined was a cell. Then I heard the door being locked.

"Confound it!" Ned shouted. I heard him bang on a wall. "These people are no better than cannibals! Well, I won't let them eat me. Not without a protest!"

"Calm yourself, Ned," Conseil said quietly. "We are not done for yet."

"Pretty near," Ned snapped. "But I have my trusty knife, and I can use it even in this darkness. I swear, the first pirate who lays a hand on me—"

"Ned, please," I protested. "Don't make matters worse with senseless violence. Maybe the crew will listen to us. We haven't even tried yet."

Ned grumbled, but he seemed calmer. I paced the dark space, trying to get a feel for its size. I could hear Conseil doing the same. I had just banged into a table when the room filled with a bright light. I squinted up at the source. It was a polished half-globe in the ceiling. This amazing ship was equipped with electricity!

"At last we can see!" Ned said.

"But we are still in the dark about our circumstances," I pointed out.

The door opened, and two men entered. I was now able to study our hosts more carefully. Their uniforms bore no resemblance to those worn by any known navy. The fabric was also unfamiliar. The taller man carried himself with such authority I knew instantly he must be the captain of this strange vessel. It was to him I addressed my comments.

"Sir," I said. "We are grateful for your hospitality."

I shot a quieting look at Ned. He gritted his teeth, but stayed silent. I introduced each of us in turn, and stated our professions. "We were traveling aboard the *Abraham Lincoln*," I explained. "When, well, hm . . ."

I realized mentioning the attack might not score points with the captain. "Anyway, we ended up in the water. And now here."

The captain listened quietly. His soft brown eyes never left my face. They seemed intelligent and somehow sad. But he gave no indication that he understood me. He said not a word in reply. Perhaps he didn't know French, my native tongue.

"Let me try English," Ned offered. I could tell by the excited way he told the story that he was exaggerating a bit. Still, the captain said nothing.

Conseil made an attempt in German. No response. I was about to try that universal language, Pig Latin, when the two men abruptly spun on their heels and left. The door locked behind them.

"The rogues!" Ned sputtered. "We speak to them in as many languages as we can, and they don't have the manners to respond?"

"Please stay calm, Ned." I had a suspicion that this was a phrase I would find myself repeating time and again. "We should wait a bit longer before forming an opinion of the captain and the crew."

"My opinion is formed. They are rascals." Ned yanked a chair away from the table and flung himself into it.

"That may be," I admitted. "However, it would help to know where they're from."

"From the land of rogues," Ned grumbled. He grabbed the ends of his shirt and squeezed water from them.

I was torn between laughing and scolding

him. "My brave Ned, I have never seen that country on a map. Until we determine their nationality, it will be very hard to know what language to try."

"That is the disadvantage of not knowing all languages," Conseil said. "Or the disadvantage of not having one universal language for all."

Ned's stomach let out a loud growl. He pointed at it. "That's a language they should be able to understand," he shouted. "Don't they know we're hungry? And wet! And cold!" He got up and paced the small room. He grew more and more angry.

I trotted after him, trying to calm him. I was just reaching up a paw to pat him when the door opened. Ned let out a shout, then lunged at a steward. Clothing flew everywhere as the poor man flailed in Ned's powerful grip.

"Ned, stop!" I barked.

I tried to pull him from the steward. Conseil grabbed Ned's arms. We could not break Ned's hold.

A sudden command made us all freeze. "Release my steward, Mr. Land," a voice ordered. "Conseil, Professor Aronnax, thank you for trying to help."

I whirled around. It was the captain who spoke. In perfect French! Ned was so startled, he let go of the struggling steward. The steward tumbled to the floor. Conseil, of course, betrayed no sign of surprise.

The capitan leaned against a wall, waiting. For what, I was not sure. I wondered if he had regretted speaking in French. Now he could not pretend not to understand.

The steward scrambled to his feet, then stood at attention. The captain made a small sign with his hand. The steward gathered up the clothing he had been carrying and placed it on the table. Then he left the room.

"Gentlemen. I speak many languages," the captain explained. "I could have spoken to you earlier, but I needed to think about my response. Most annoying circumstances have brought you into my presence. I have broken all ties with humanity. And yet, here you are."

"By accident," I pointed out.

"Was it an accident that the *Abraham Lincoln* pursued me all over the seas? Was it an accident that you were aboard that vessel?" His voice rose, but he stayed calm. "Was it an accident that sent a cannonball my way? Or that Ned Land struck me with his harpoon?"

I raised a paw to shush Ned before he could speak. I had the perfect answers—answers that should clear the air once and for all.

"Sir," I replied. "No doubt you are unaware of the worldwide discussions concerning you. You see, because ships have collided with your vessel, several governments joined to take action. We believed we were chasing a monster. We felt it our duty to rid the seas of the dangerous creature and make the ocean safe for travel."

I smiled at the captain. I knew that as a man of reason, he would hold no grudge.

A half-smile formed on the captain's lips, but it wasn't a friendly expression. "Monsieur Aronnax, do you dare claim that the captain of the *Abraham Lincoln* would have not attacked if he knew this was a ship—and not a monster?"

I was about to argue, then realized he was right. If Commander Farragut had discovered this submarine, he would have pursued it with even greater determination.

The captain nodded at my silence. "Then you understand why I may treat you as enemies. Nothing obliges me to extend you any hospitality. I could have left you riding atop our submarine. It would have been my right."

"The right of a savage, perhaps," Ned shouted. "Not of a civilized man."

"I am not what you call a civilized man," the captain snapped. "I have rejected society. I do not obey its laws."

I gulped. What kind of man are we dealing with? I wondered. The captain admitted he was bound by no law. He was responsible to no one but himself. Our lives would be determined by his conscience.

"I may not believe in society," the man continued. "But I do believe in the rights of human beings. Therefore I have come to a decision. Fate has brought you here. So here you remain. But you must agree to one condition."

"What is it?" I asked.

"It is possible that on occasion I will need to confine you to your rooms," the captain explained. "You will obey without question. If you agree, you will have freedom."

I glanced at Ned and Conseil. Conseil nodded, and Ned glowered. "We agree," I answered for them. "But I have a question. You say we'll have freedom. What kind of freedom do you mean?"

The captain shrugged. "Free to enjoy yourselves on board as any other member of my crew. Except, of course, in those rare circumstances I just spoke of."

"But this is only the freedom a prisoner has in his prison!" I protested.

"It will have to do."

"Do you mean we have to give up ever seeing our countries, our friends, our families again?" I demanded.

"Of course," the captain replied evenly. "Giving up the world is not so difficult. I have been far happier since I did."

"I will not give you my word of honor that

I won't escape," Ned declared.

The captain studied him coldly. "I did not ask for your word of honor, Mr. Land."

"This is too much!" I exclaimed.

The captain's dark eyes flashed with anger. "Perhaps you're right. I give you too much. I could have dropped you into the ocean. After all, you attacked me. You arrive uninvited and discover a secret I have worked terribly hard to protect. I cannot and will not allow you to leave."

"So you give us a choice between your kind of life, or death," I said.

"Exactly."

I turned to Ned and Conseil. "Well, friends, when the choice is put that way, there is only one answer." I faced the mysterious captain again. "We agree to your terms. But no word of honor binds us to the master of this vessel."

"None," the captain agreed.

I sat back on my haunches. "You know our names. How shall we address you?"

"You may call me Captain Nemo. You and your friends are passengers on my submarine, the *Nautilus*."

Nemo. How fitting, I thought. The word Nemo meant "no one" in Latin. So I was talking to Captain Nobody. He really did want to keep his identity a secret.

The captain smiled. "You may find life aboard *Nautilus* quite pleasant. Particularly you, Professor."

I cocked an ear. Did Captain Nemo know of my interest in marine biology?

"I've read your book," Captain Nemo continued. "I admire it—as far as you were able to go. Now you are going to see sights you haven't even dreamed of. We are going into a world of marvels."

Pierre was thrilled by the opportunity to explore the ocean. My friends and I are also eager to explore Aqua-Land during our visit in Florida. Don't miss the exciting outcome of all these voyages in Twenty Thousand Wags Under the Sea, *the next book in the Adventures of Wishbone™ series.*

WISHBONE Mysteries

Read all the books in the
WISHBONE™ Mysteries series!

The Adventures of WISHBONE™

Read all the books in
The Adventures of Wishbone™ series!

Coming Soon!

#20

Wishbone Mysteries

The Wishbone Mysteries

CASE OF THE BREAKING STORY

The Goldale Chronicle

WISHBONE ON THE TRAIL OF MISSING STATUE

CANINE

By Alexander Steele